Little Reminders of Who I Was

Also by Jeff S. Bray

The Five Barred Gate
The Transference
Little Reminders of Who I Am

Little Reminders
of Who I Was

Jeff S. Bray

WordCrafts Press

Little Reminders of Who I Was is a work of fiction. The author has endeavored to be as accurate as possible with regard to the times and place in which the events of this novel is set. Still, this is a novel, and all references to persons, places, and events are fictitious or are used fictitiously.

Little Reminders of Who I Was
Copyright © 2022
Jeff S. Bray

ISBN: 978-1-957344-46-1

Cover art by Carolyn Bray at Colorful Creations by Carolyn
Cover design by David Warren

Published by WordCrafts Press
Cody, Wyoming 82414
www.wordcrafts.net

Prologue

Three years ago

Carter walked around the corner of the last apartment structure and into the city park. The sun was rising, casting its beam across the grass. It sent a plume of steam off the chilled ground. He continued across a path and through a bank of trees when a voice drew his attention.

"Impressive, Carter. You performed above and beyond expectations. He is grateful for your hard work," Gabriel said, then added with a smile, "I knew I could count on you for this."

"Was there ever a doubt?" Carter said, humor evident in his voice.

"Never," said Gabriel, returning the jest. They both laughed.

Carter walked on a little farther—Gabriel followed. A short distance later, he sat on a bench that overlooked the city. "People amaze me. They go about living their lives in a rush, and they seem to ignore the very reason they're rushing around. I don't understand how they can be so preoccupied with nothing at all. It doesn't seem like it's worth it when you consider the big picture. If I had a nervous bone in my body, it would be very unnerved."

"That's what we are here for," Gabriel reassured. "To remind them."

The two angels sat and watched men and women from each walk of life begin their day, oblivious to their people-watching activity.

Gabriel looked up to the sky and squinted. "It's going to be a nice day."

"That's what they say," said Carter.

"So," Gabriel said, as he stood and looked down at Carter, "are you ready for your next assignment?"

Carter looked up into Gabriel's blazing blue eyes and smiled.

Today

"Gabriel, it's good to see you. What brings you my way this lovely evening," Carter said, leaning back on his park bench, watching a couple of squirrels fight over a fallen nut.

"I have something that may interest you," the angel with crystal blue eyes said, sitting beside him. He held another shoebox; the way Carter preferred his cases handled.

"It's not like the last one, is it?" Carter began. "I enjoyed bringing the Harveys together, and I understand it was His work, but it just felt routine. I haven't felt challenged in a while."

"What, you want something like Aaron and Deborah?" Gabriel said with his eyebrows raised.

Carter knew his friend too well. Something was up by his cutting to the chase so quickly. "That was three years ago. Why would you bring them up? What is He up to this time?"

"Why does God have to be up to something to send me to you and ask you about a case?"

"Because I know Him so well. And I know you, Gabe," Carter said and stood with his hand outstretched. "Let me see the box."

"It won't tell you anything," Gabriel said, handing him the same beat-up shoebox Carter had always used for the past unknown years he had been his overseer.

Carter sat and removed the cover. He tilted his tweed hat back, and his silver eyebrows furrowed as he looked over the various items. He didn't place any of them. None struck a chord or made any sense to him. He looked up to Gabriel.

"I told you. Just follow the instructions and place them as He leads you to place them. Same as always. Other leadings will follow. You know how this works."

"What's the catch?" Carter asked, lowering his hat. "What do Aaron and Deborah have to do with this case?"

"Who said they did?"

"You did. Why would you bring them up if they had nothing to do with this case?"

"Okay, you got me," Gabriel sighed. "When was the last time you visited Houston?"

"The night you gave me the Johnson case. I haven't had the pleasure of visiting since. Beautiful library downtown. Architecture, ambiance, and a café with all the coffee you can drink. They have a late-night—"

Gabriel cut him off, "Wonderful, wonderful. What do you think about grabbing your next cup of joe at that café?"

"I'm going back to Houston?"

"As the Lord directs," Gabriel says. "Well, not Houston directly. A bit further south of there. A city called Sunnyside. But your assignment works in Houston."

"A he this time?"

"Yes."

"It's about time," Carter sighed, "It'll feel good to be back building some male camaraderie. I have you, but no offense, you're not someone I can sit and watch a baseball game with."

"None taken. I'm a football fan anyhow."

The joke made Carter laugh. "Heh. I should've known. Saints, right?"

Both men laughed.

"Okay. Let's get back to the task. How long?" Carter asked.

Gabriel looked up at the crisp sky, then to Carter. "Two months. Your first placement needs to be accomplished tomorrow by 12:30. Other than that, you are free to place as you see fit."

"Tomorrow in Houston? He does realize we're in Seattle?" Carter said.

"You let Him worry about the details. You just accept the assignment."

"Understood, boss," Carter said. "Anything else?"

"Be prepared for anything. Remember, God is in control. No matter what happens, know that He is with you and will see you through any struggle you face."

Carter nodded as he stood. Lifting his shoebox, he bid his visitor farewell.

Chapter
One

"Would you care to sign up for our email list, Mr. John-son?" Derrick Anders asked the customer across from him.

"No, son, I'm already a member," the white-haired Mr. Johnson said with his eyes furrowed. "If you'd look at your screen, you'd know that." He grabbed the bag with his book, *How to Win Friends and Influence People*, and walked away in a huff.

Derrick apologized with a smile as Mr. Johnson exited the bookstore. He greeted the next customer with as much energy as he had with the older gentleman. The system told him her name was Penny Clawson. Penny's customer account email was filled in, unlike Mr. Johnson's. The screen wouldn't prompt him to ask, and he wouldn't be embarrassed as he was five minutes ago.

The line dwindled, and Derrick took the stack of returns behind him and began to load them onto his restocking cart. These were the books customers had second thoughts about or didn't have enough money for. Derrick was always amazed at the prices on the register screen. But it was his job to confirm the author's worthiness as well as the establishment's justification for charging that price.

Although Derrick worked at a bookstore, he wasn't an avid reader. The most he read were his college textbooks. Even then, it was just enough to get a passing grade. In high school, it had been his mom who persuaded him to pay attention. Between those mom-induced grades and academic scholarships he got into a decent college. With those scholarship funds and his job at the bookstore he was getting by.

Not long after Derrick started college, the unthinkable happened—his mom passed away. Derrick had to grow up overnight. There was supposed to be a will leaving him the house, but no one seemed to know whether it actually existed, or if it did, where it was. Either way, the house came to him. Along with the mortgage—that was a whole other story. Between paying bills and college, when all was said and done, he felt spread thin. It was quite a bit for the shoulders of a nineteen-year-old. Almost enough to drive one to drink, and he wasn't even old enough for a sip.

Two years later, he was doing much better. The roof was still over his head, and the lights were still on. He had fixed up a Toyota in high school as soon as he received his license and had driven it since. It was paid for, and insurance was almost a joke since the vehicle was a standard. With his clean record and now being twenty-one, his rates were fairly low. It was one of the blessings he thanked the Lord for as he drove through his Sunnyside community to his job at the local chain bookseller.

Derrick wheeled his loaded cart down the Crime Fiction aisle, returning books to the shelf. He turned around to see a dark-haired woman staring at him. Derrick sighed. "Hey, Breonna."

"Hi, Derrick," Breonna said, handing him a copy of *L.A. Confidential.* Keven Spacey and Kim Bassinger stared at him. He looked at it as she continued, "That's not the original cover. They redid it after the movie came out. The novel by James Eloy was written years before the movie came out."

"Is that right?" Derrick said. He had heard of the movie and knew the actors but could care less there was a book about the film.

"Yep. Most of the books in this section have been made into movies. *The Silence of the Lambs, Psycho*, and I'm sure you know almost everything by Stephen King is a movie nowadays."

Derrick nodded and placed a couple more books on the shelves, even one by Stephen King—*The Gun Slinger*. He didn't ask Breonna about it because he didn't want a lecture about the old west or a Siskel and Ebert review. "That's interesting. You must love books to know so much."

"You know me," Breonna shrugged with a smile, which Derrick had to admit was pleasant. "Well, I gotta get back to work. Talk with ya later."

Derrick returned to the front counter and finished his day with a couple more Mr. Johnsons but more Patty Clawsons, making his job tolerable. Every now and then, Breonna would pop her head around the corner to say hello, taking returns for restocking, more books that customers second-guessed themselves on. By closing time, his size 12s hurt, and his mind was exhausted.

After counting out his till, part of his tasks were to stock up bags and straighten shelves across the front of the store. When the manager finally locked the doors behind everyone, his car seat welcomed him. Derrick drove home to his textbooks, waiting for a night of studying. Midterms were next week. Tired or not, studying was on tonight's agenda.

Derrick woke to the sound of his alarm. It was the same alarm his mom woke to on countless mornings for her nursing job. That squawking noise was one of the things that made him proud of her because despite what life threw at them, she'd always get up when it sounded and faced her day head-on. While they never lived in luxury, they did pretty well—well enough that his mom chose to become a homeowner. He was amazed the bank gave her the loan—a single black mother in South Houston with a meager job. *God has His hand on us,* she would always say. And He must have, because the house was there, and the lights and gas were always on. Derrick had no complaints—until the day God took her from him.

There were issues with paying for the house. After his mom passed, he continued to make payments, but he had no idea how much he still owed on the home. He knew the mortgage was auto-drafted, so he kept funding his mom's account, but the bank gave him issues. They wouldn't allow him to do anything with the account other than make deposits. Their reasoning was he had to be a cosigner. They told him to bring her in so she could add him. Derrick reminded them repeatedly that she had passed away. "Well, sir, then you will have to wait until the account is closed and then attempt to request any funds after it hits probate." He couldn't even find out if his mom left a balance. His only option was to deposit the amount of the mortgage to keep them happy and a roof over his head.

Derrick's morning shower was cold because the water

heater was acting up again. Another thing to add to the list of things going wrong. After his ice bath and beard trim, he checked the clock. If he hurried, he had enough time for a quick breakfast at the corner taco shop. He had class this morning, and if he wanted to beat the traffic, he needed to leave now for the shop around the corner.

A bell sounded when he opened the door to Maria's Cocina. Gary, a regular, was sitting in the corner nursing a cup of coffee. He had been a fixture since Derrick began eating at the restaurant. He was a 60-year-old Gulf War veteran with a love of sugar, going by the number of empty packets that surrounded his coffee cup.

"I can't believe Porter missed that shot last night," Gary said, taking a sip from his steaming cup.

"You can't make them all," Derrick said, looking up at the wall menu. "Plus, he's coming back from the DL."

"Yeah, I suppose."

"Did you go out to see it?"

"Out? No man, I was there," Gary said, taking his eyes off his cup and meeting Derrick's stare.

"Yeah?"

"Yeah. Another member of the Lion's Club had tickets and called me at the last minute. Lower level, center court."

"Nice," Derrick said, nodding. "Well, at least they won."

"Yeah. But OT." Gary said, his head lowered to his cup, shaking. "If Porter hadn't missed that shot."

"True," Derrick couldn't help but smile and laugh to himself.

Derrick's order was called. He bid his sulking friend farewell and headed out the door, where he would begin his hopefully traffic-free drive to the college.

Like his mom, Derrick wanted to help people. His field of

study was social services. He had heard stories of what it was like not to have family support. He and his mom had been alone, but they were making it. She would tell him stories of those who came into the clinic who had nothing and remind him of how blessed they were. Her passion was the drive he needed to succeed in school. After she passed, that drive wavered a bit, but his passion remained, maybe even grew.

The most challenging part of school for Derrick was the first year and a half of prerequisites. Now that he was in his third year, he was knee-deep in the meat and potatoes of his education. His schedule consisted of classes with topics such as Psychology and Parent and Child Relationships. The latter he had been nervous about taking. What if they discussed his situation? He wasn't sure he was prepared to talk about his mom yet, let alone the circumstances surrounding her death. He hoped for textbook and educational learning and not so much practical application. So far, so good.

Tuesday's course schedule went by faster than he had expected. Derrick felt more confident about midterms. By the time his English professor excused them for the day, his mind was already on work and getting through his shift to get home to study. He didn't want to lose momentum and needed to pull at least an 80 average to keep his academic advisor happy and the scholarship funding coming in. He was ready to clock in and complete his shift.

The moment he pulled into the lot, he knew the day was not going to be what he had said a silent prayer for. The sign in the window told the whole story. Tuesdays were when new releases hit the shelves, thus also when new sales went into effect. A new book from the suspense-thriller master himself, Stephen King, was hitting the shelves. And a romance novel from an author whose name he could not pronounce—nor cared to learn how to—arrived with the obligatory promo posters—a bare-chested male with a woman's arm draped around him from behind.

Derrick pulled into his usual spot, out and away from customer parking—company policy. It was not as busy as it appeared when he entered, but the smell of coffee draped its presence around him from the shop that adjoined the store. He wasn't sure why he didn't like coffee, but the aroma turned his nose. Perhaps the father he never got to know was a drinker of the stuff, or maybe it was the man in the hat? He had found a cup of coffee on the kitchen table one morning after he saw his mom arguing with him. He never saw the man again, and his mom was not a coffee drinker. That was almost four years ago. He'd hated coffee ever since.

"Good morning, Derrick," an older man behind the counter called. "There are pastries in the breakroom. And a voucher for a free coffee next door. Amelia sent them over."

"Thanks, Mr. Lauder," Derrick said to his boss. He walked to the back and snagged a raspberry danish, but passed on the free coffee tickets. After punching in his four-digit code at the kiosk, he was ready to start the day. Derrick passed through the swinging doors into the Mystery and Adventure section and ran into the girl with the pleasant smile.

"Good morning, Derrick," Breonna said, her smile lighting up any hidden mystery and definitely taking him on an adventure.

"Hey, Breonna. How are you?" Derrick said, trying to avoid eye contact. He knew she was attracted to him. Everyone did, but he didn't feel that way, and the last thing he needed right now was to be distracted by a relationship. As she spoke of her evening's studies, his eyes drifted to the books upon the shelf, the posters on the wall, to the headband she wore. Derrick's eyes locked on the hairpiece. It looked familiar—too familiar.

"Breonna," Derrick stopped her mid-sentence about her phlebotomy studies. "Where did you get that headband?"

Breonna's eyes lit up, her smile hiding them. "Do you like it? I love the pattern. It's unique, isn't it?"

"Yes, it is. Where did you get it?" Derrick asked again.

"I found it at a rummage sale at the Catholic church over on Third. Why?"

"I think that's my mom's headband?"

"Your mom's? Are you sure?" Breonna said, reaching for the band.

"Positive. That pattern is unique. I know because she made it."

"Oh my," Breonna said, removing the hairpiece. "Well, I want to give it back to her. How did she lose it?"

"You—can't give it back to her."

"Why not?"

Derrick's eyes began to tear up. Breonna saw it, and she knew.

"Oh. I'm sorry. When did she pass away?"

"About three years ago. My aunt took most of the things out of the house and either sold them or donated them."

"I'm so sorry," Breonna said, putting her hand on Derrick's arm and holding out the headband. "Do you want it?"

Derrick shook his head. "No, you keep it. I know she would be happy it went to someone who appreciated its beauty. Besides, it looks good on you."

Breonna's smile returned with Derrick's words, and she replaced the band in her hair. "Thank you. I felt a bond with it the minute I saw it. The vendor said it was made special for me. He was such a kind man."

Chapter
Two

Derrick found it difficult to focus on his studies that evening; he couldn't get his mom's headband out of his head. They had been donated over three years ago. His aunt boxed up the house without any concern for what she was doing. He watched her pack up his mom's favorite blouses and the hair accessories she would create. *Did she realize how hard she worked on them?* the teenager asked himself.

Derrick looked around the room. His home was much smaller now, and it was his responsibility. His aunt moved back to San Antonio and left him in charge of it all, including what was left of the phantom mortgage. She claimed she didn't have the paperwork, but why would she lie about something like that? He was okay with making the payments and glad the bank was at least allowing him to deposit into the account. But how long would that last? He needed to find the paperwork. Which reminded him, he had paperwork of his own to attend to. He looked down at his Family Studies assignment, which was still a blur, and tossed his pencil onto the table.

"This is a waste of time," Derrick said aloud, picking up his phone. He dialed and waited.

An excited voice answered, "Hey D'rick, what's shakin'?"

Jarrod had called him D'rick, or some other variation of his name, since high school. Some days it was *Ricky*, others it was just plain *D*. Derrick could tell his mood by the name he was being called. It was a tell that Jarrod had. Today he was in a good mood, which made Derrick glad. It was just what he needed at the moment.

"Hey, Jarrod. Watcha up to?"

"About to head to the shop. The old man got his hands on a Packard. A Packard! Can you believe it? We've been waiting to get under the hood of one of those beauties for years," his friend beamed.

"Sounds like a fun time. I won't keep you then," Derrick said, trying not to let his disappointment reflect in his voice.

"Alright, hit me up later. We'll get together. God bless," Jarrod said and hung up, not giving him a chance to respond.

Derrick laughed. He envied the relationship Jarrod had with his father. It seemed they were always under the hood of a vehicle in the shop his dad owned. It had been in the family since his grandfather owned it in the 1940s. And a black man owning anything during that time period was unheard of. He had heard stories of it being nearly being burned down twice. But it still stood today. Derrick remembered seeing photographs in the office and waiting area of how it looked through the ages—it hadn't changed much. Rundown, but that only led to its charm and how his father liked it.

Derrick was young when his father passed away. His *father* was young when he passed away. He had just celebrated his twenty-second birthday and first wedding anniversary.

Derrick couldn't talk or walk, much less remember a face, but as his mom explained it, he was his pride and joy. He would come home from the office, and even before he'd put his keys down, he had Derrick in his arms. However, as time moved on, she spoke less and less of him, until he eventually became a *remember when.*

After he died, she spent every waking moment working to keep a roof over their heads. She was a waitress in a diner working whatever shift they'd schedule her until a regular in for a late dinner noticed her determination. Dr. Keller encouraged her to attend nursing school. She didn't listen at first, but after further encouragement, his mom looked into it. She found an online campus and later a sitter for him so she could attend in person. A year and a half later, she was taking her exit exam.

Derrick wasn't sure where the financing came from, but through paying for his own education now, he assumed she also had student loans and different grants. With the way his mom spoke of Dr. Keller, he wouldn't have been surprised to find her hand behind some of the funding. She, too, was a doctor who had to face the challenges of becoming who she was at the time. His mom spoke of her fondly. However, if his mom did have student loans, they must've been paid off because that was one bill he'd never seen.

Not having education bills probably helped them have a nicer house. He liked it because he had his own room, and it was huge—well, to a five-year-old with his first room it was huge. His room was on the second floor. The staircase was unique because it had two small flights of stairs with a landing in the middle. One of Derrick's favorite pastimes was climbing down the first flight and sitting on the landing wrapped in his blanket and watching his mom cook breakfast. He smiled as he remembered all the breakfasts they'd shared. Then he frowned because that landing was also where he saw the man in the hat three years ago.

Derrick closed his eyes, took a deep breath, and released it and the memories. "Okay, I need to get back to this report." He picked up his pencil and looked over his study material. His current assignment was to write a paper on the relationship between parent and child and how society plays a part in their development. This paper was one he had been dreading. He read it on the professor's syllabus and knew it was coming. Now it was here. And he would have to deal with it or fail this class. And failure was not an option.

Writing papers was never an issue for Derrick. Getting started was the problem. Once the boulder of his brain got rolling, there was no stopping it. He hoped that would be the case here; he just needed to find the lever that would lift this stone and get it rolling. Should he center this piece on all his mom did, or the lack of a father and him having to step up? Derrick stared up at the popcorn ceiling. It brought back the worries of Jarrod telling him of the dangers of asbestos. He didn't know anything about it, but he said he could have his uncle, who was a carpenter, look into it, taking a sample from the bedroom.

"Derrick," he said again to himself, "Focus!" He sat up in his chair and woke up his computer. The beep echoed, and the blank document laughed while the curser danced in amusement. He was reminded that his mom always said, *Remain positive no matter how dire the situation may seem. And always find the good in the bad.* He knew how he should approach this assignment. Half an hour later, he was well on his way. Two hours later, he had a term paper rough draft complete.

The clock on the wall told him he needed to be up in six hours for class, to his benefit, not this course. Even so, Professor Adkins was not looking for this paper until next week. He had until then to revise or change his mind about leaving his father out of it completely. Derrick's eyes crossed from the strain, and he pinched the bridge of his nose and exhaled.

"Okay, that's over," he told the screen, shutting the computer down.

After a glass of water and evening routines, he headed to his room—which used to be his mom's room. It took him nearly a year to allow himself to sleep in her bed. It just felt strange to him. But after a long conversation, Jarrod convinced him that his mom would feel dishonored if he remained in the child's room sleeping in a child's bed. She worked hard for it. She worked hard for him. That night he packed his pillow and comforter and made the move.

Derrick closed his laptop after his Personal Development professor concluded his lecture and dismissed the class. He made a mad dash to his car; Wednesdays were the worst on his schedule, with class out at 1:00 and his shift starting at 2:00. His building was furthest from the parking lot, and post-lunch traffic was the worst. The minute he hit the ground floor, he knew he would be late; the students entering the building shaking off umbrellas told him so.

Derrick sighed aloud, drawing the attention of a couple of freshmen heading up the stairs. From the looks on their faces, he could've let out a growl. He nodded in apology and stepped into the soggy crowd and the sounds of squealing sneakers. Once out of the building, it wasn't as bad as it seemed, just a passing shower, but even so, the roads would be wet. He resigned to the delay and walked the rest of the way to his car.

It was just before 2:30 when he pulled into the lot at the bookstore. It was dry in this part of town. He just hoped that his boss paid attention to the weather reports. Brian, another worker, nodded as he entered the building; Derrick shrugged and raised his hand in apology. He hurried to the kiosk, clocked in, and back to the front to the waiting line of customers.

"Can I help who's next?" Derrick called to the next person in line. He was a white-haired gentleman in a tweed jacket and matching hat.

"Good afternoon," the man said. "You look to be in a rush this morning."

"Yes. Caught in one of those Houston pop-up showers on my way in."

"Yes, I know how those can be. I get caught in quite a few of them myself." The man grinned, nodding toward the window. It was raining again.

"No umbrella?" Derrick asked.

"Never saw the need. I generally find the shelter I need when it's required."

"Well, that's good. So, how can I help you today, sir?"

"I'm looking for a particular book. I've looked through your shelves, but I can't seem to find it."

"What's the title and author?" Derrick asked, bringing his terminal to life.

"It's by an older author. Her name is Elanor Strong. The book is titled *Angel's Among Us.*"

Derrick's eyes froze on the screen. He hadn't keyed in a single word of the man's request. He turned and met the man's stare. "Sir, how do you know that book?"

"The question is, how do you, Derrick?"

"My mom used to read it to me when I was little. It's filled with stories of people who had encounters with angels. She would tell me we never know who we may come across in life and that we should be kind to every soul we meet."

"Wise counsel," the man beamed. "Entertaining angels unaware."

"Exactly the phrase she used," Derrick's face lit up.

"It's one of my favorites as well. I was at the library, and it seems their only copy has been checked out. I was hoping you sold it here. It's such a fabulous book that I wanted to own my own copy."

"You can't," Derrick said a bit too quickly. "Sorry, I meant, it's out of print. Has been for years. I don't even think it was in print when my mom read it to me. The stories are from folks in the 1950s and '60s. It's an old book too, faded green covering, gold-lettered spine."

"Yes, before both of our times," the man chuckled. "Beautiful book, though."

"That it was," Derrick smiled at the recognition. He wished he had his copy as well. Another one of those items that had disappeared when his aunt took over. His hope now was that some child was getting the encouragement he received from it. "Well, I'm sorry we couldn't help. Hopefully, the person who checked it out will return it soon. Is there anything else I can help you find?"

"I think that'll be enough for today, Derrick. It was a pleasure meeting you and hearing your story. I'm usually at the

Houston Library downtown if you ever want to chat. It's the best in town."

"I'll keep that in mind, sir. You have a great day." Derrick said.

The visitor tipped his hat and smiled.

Derrick turned to the next customer, "Can I help who's next?"

Chapter
Three

Derrick received a stern warning for his tardiness from Mr. Lauder. He pleaded his case but still was told that further violations of company policy would result in disciplinary action—the typical boss-speech learned during training and repeated verbatim so an employee would shape up.

"You're a great employee, Derrick." Mr. Lauder began, pushing his thick-rimmed glasses up his nose. "I don't want to write you up. But I would be setting a bad example if another employee saw your tardiness with no consequences. So, I'll let today slide, but if it happens again, we'll need to put it on paper."

"I understand, Mr. Lauder. I'm sorry. It won't happen again." Derrick wasn't convinced his statement was completely accurate. It may have reflected in his voice from the less than satisfied look Mr. Lauder gave him.

"Okay," he said, nodding. "Go ahead and get back to work. There should be a rack of returns ready to go."

"I'm on it," Derrick said and left the office before his boss could think of a punishment fitting his crime.

Returns were no big deal. It kept him moving. Standing behind the register was something he didn't enjoy. It wasn't that he didn't like customer interaction—it was the lack of movement. He wasn't your average twenty-something. He was built more like a defensive lineman. Standing stationary behind the register made him uncomfortable.

Once back on the store's sales floor, he came across Simon, who worked in the Fiction section. He had a curious smirk on his face.

"Hey, Simon."

"Hey, Derrick," Simon said, then proceeded with his exploration of Derrick's appearance.

After a couple of steps, Derrick stopped and snapped, "What?"

"Nothing. Just looking for where Lauder ripped your new one."

"It wasn't *that* bad," Derrick laughed. "If it happens again, I get written up. He understood it wasn't completely my fault."

"Yeah, well, it would be bad for you to leave, considering."

"Considering what?"

"You know. Breonna."

"What about her?"

"Dude. Everyone knows she likes you," Simon said.

"Yeah, well, I'm not interested in any relationship with anyone right now. Especially at work."

"Just thought you should know. She's a sweet girl. Be careful," Simon said, his voice gaining an edge to it.

"I'll keep that in mind, but I doubt she's interested. She's friendly with everyone. Even you, Simon."

"Hey. I'm off the market. My girl would have my head in a sack if I were to even look at another girl."

As if on cue, a customer called over to them. Her son was looking for a *History of King Louis XVI.* The two men exchanged glances and burst into laughter, leaving the customer clueless. Both had to apologize, and Derrick could hear Simon explaining his story and the history of Louis and Marie Antoinette as he led the customer back into his section.

Derrick looked toward the Non-Fiction section, Breonna's department. He didn't see her or her smile anywhere. He considered a quick shortcut until he remembered it was Wednesday and that she didn't work today. During tonight's cart trips, she wouldn't be peeking around corners to say hello or give him a quick fact about one of the books he was shelving. With the realization, he felt reluctant to finish his shift.

For the rest of the day, Derrick paid extra attention to each book he placed on the shelf. Occasionally he would read the description on the back of the book if the cover grabbed his attention, wondering if Breonna had read it or if she had a story to tell about the book. He had told Simon he had no interest in pursuing a relationship with her, and that was the truth. His schedule was too full to squeeze in personal time. And Breonna was friendly with everyone she encountered, not just him. Her niceness was just who she was. It didn't necessarily mean she liked him.

Derrick shook off his derailed train of thought, it had slowed his pace. The last thing he needed was a second reprimand in one afternoon. This only proved his point—a relationship would only complicate his situation. He needed to focus on his studies, work, and keeping order in his life. A relationship would disrupt that order, especially one at work.

The rest of his day went by slowly. With the lack of customers, he was assigned to dusting and zoning shelves in

Fitness and Nutrition. He had to laugh at the covers and display advertisements for some of them. Never in a million years would he ever look like any of them. No amount of dieting or exercise could save his large frame. But some felt that his size was an advantage. The coaches in high school practically begged him to try out for the football team. They told him sports would allow him to write his own future. But he never felt an attraction to sports, so he never tried out.

That was another thing he loved about his mother—she never pushed him to do anything he didn't want to do. She did remind him of the opportunities before him, but he explained that he wanted to focus on his academics, nothing more. To her benefit, she left it at that. And even though he didn't graduate with spectacular grades, he did receive scholarships, which were helping pay for his schooling now. He paid little out of pocket. And he didn't have to throw a ball to do it.

Now he was in his junior year and managed to earn decent grades while studying social work. He wanted to help people living through the situation he grew up in. For most of his life he only had one parent as his mom never remarried or even dated, for that matter. He did have a babysitter while his mom worked. Sister Georgia was also his Sunday School teacher at the church they attended when they were able. He grew up with her for the majority of his adolescence.

Sister Georgia was great, but she was older and more a grandmother figure than anything. She could bake a mean upside-down cake, too. Derrick loved the monthly meal at the church because she would make it every time. He remembered always trying to sneak a piece before eating the main meal, but as responsible moms are, he had to finish everything on his plate before getting in line for the desserts. Cakes were Sister Georgia's expertise, but advice for a growing child? That was not her forte. For parental guidance, he needed his mom, but now she was gone.

The experience of not having a parental figure around filled him with the desire to help others like himself. She had that drive; he inherited it. It must've come from her. He never knew his father or heard enough about him to know what type of person he was. And Derrick never considered asking to find out. He always thought there would be time. Now he'd never know.

He finished his straightening with a diet book from a nutritionist that looked bigger than he did. He had to laugh at the irony. When he finally made his way to the front, the lights in the parking lot revealed less than a dozen cars, half of which were the employees. Brian was standing at the register on his phone, probably texting with his girlfriend who was just getting off work about now. They were engaged and going to be married at the end of the year.

Derrick pushed his cart toward the register and saw Mr. Lauder coming from the periodical section. He cleared his throat as a warning to Brian, who picked up the hint, tucked his phone into his pocket, and went back to straightening the front register snack displays. He nodded to Derrick and crossed behind the registers with his empty cart.

"Thanks," Brian said after Mr. Lauder passed them and walked down the aisle toward the back of the store.

Derrick nodded.

"Penny is looking at floral displays for the wedding. She was sending me samples to look at," he explained.

"Not too much longer now. Just a few more months."

"I know. Penny is so excited. Every little planning detail, she sends me photos. Last week it was the bridesmaids' corsages."

"She's having fun," Derrick laughed.

"Yes, she is. I love it," Brian said, his eyes lighting up. "I'll admit, these details I could care less about, but she's so into it, I can't help but get excited with her."

"Well, I'm happy for you. I hope someday to be just as happy," Derrick said, but as soon as he did, wish he hadn't. He knew he'd opened the door.

"Well, you know, Derrick, you could have happiness staring you in the face."

"Not you too?" Derrick said, not looking up, feigning dusting the counter.

"It's no secret that Breonna is into you."

"So I've heard."

"And you not?"

"It's not like that. I just have too much on my plate to think about a relationship."

"So, you *are* interested in her?" Brian asked, a little too interested.

"Even if I am, it doesn't matter. I just don't think it would be a good idea to date a coworker."

"Suit yourself," Brian shrugged. "I don't think she would shut you down if you would at least talk to her."

Derrick knew Brian was right. She wouldn't. He wanted to take the chance, but he was fighting to keep his grades up as it was, and he didn't need them to suffer any further. If he were to begin to see Breonna and his grades dropped further, he would do what he needed to do to keep his grades up, which could mean neglecting her. And that would be worse than not asking her out to begin with. Yeah, he had to stick with his original premise. Love would have to wait. His future depended on it. The kids whom he would help in that future depended on it. Breonna's heart depended on it.

The two of them finished cleaning the front of the store without further talk of love or relationships. The Astros were doing well in the play-offs. It looked as if their team would advance to the next round. Just like Gary and the Rockets, Derrick could talk baseball with Brandon. While he never played either sport, he enjoyed watching and talking both. The great American pastimes were part of his Sunday afternoon wind down.

By the time Derrick arrived home, it was past ten, but he still had the final edit on his Parent-Child Development assignment to complete. He fixed a sandwich, grabbed a soda, and started his computer. The familiar Windows chime and default background image greeted him. He wasn't one for flash or gimmick. Even his phone had its blue splash default screen with just the time ticking away. He never saw the point of using a background image on his phone. His mind wandered from the nothing on his screen, and he wondered what image would be on Breonna's phone. He saw her smile again and had to shake it from his mind.

"Great, Derrick," he said to himself. "Good luck getting any work done tonight."

Four

Derrick found the focus he needed to complete his paper and was able to get four solid hours of sleep before his alarm urged him out of the comfort of his bed. Another quick shower, that was thankfully warm today, and a glance in the mirror, and he was out the door, triple-checking his bag for his flash drive. He left a bit earlier than usual because he had to print out his paper for Professor Adkins at the on-campus library.

The bell chimed as Derrick entered the taco shop, and Gary, on cue, shouts, "Altuuuve!"

"Guess you saw the game?" Derrick laughed.

"You didn't?" Gary said, tipping his Stros cap, so Derrick was sure to notice it.

"Naw, I had to work," Derrick said, placing his order. "But I heard it was memorable. A coworker was keeping an eye on it through an app on his phone."

"Yeah, it was good. My buddies and I were over at the Hall where we have a big screen. Max grilled, and we had a blast."

"Sound's great. You think the Dodgers will make it again? They're breezing through."

"Pssshh. L.A.," Gary said, waving his hand through the air, "We've beaten them already. We have nothing to prove. Bring on the next team."

Derrick received his order. "Guess we'll see. Good to see you, Gary."

"Yeah, you too. Be safe out there," Gary said, raising his coffee cup.

Derrick returned the gesture as the bell sounded his exit.

Leaving earlier put him in line with the tail end of morning rush hour, and there was a bit more congestion than he was used to on Calhaven. Derrick sat behind a Subaru doing twenty-five causing red marks on his paper to dance in his mind. Professor Adkins was known for lowering grades based on tardiness, and this was one paper he wanted to pull at least an eighty-five on. His advisor also had warned him about keeping his average up. Checking his mirror, he switched lanes, praying for green lights up to and through the park.

Traffic was one thing that his mom had mastered. She could get anywhere in the city in record time. It was one thing that he felt he, too, had down fairly well. Perhaps it was inborn, passed on at birth, or maybe it was a prayer his mom said over his Toyota. Some days, he was able to weave through traffic with ease and make it to places in record time like the vehicle had a mind of its own. Then, of course, there were days like yesterday when he would be thirty minutes late. But of course, it was always about safety. Maybe, the car knew that as well. Today he needed his precision model to guide him through the city and get him to the University of Houston and a passing grade.

The student library was quiet but busy as usual. Students were preparing for midterms. Many were in the same boat he was in, completing term papers. He passed a study group, a couple that was more interested in each other than studying, and a guy who looked like he had been there most of the night with bloodshot eyes and three emptied cans of Red Bull.

The clock told him he had twenty minutes to get to class. Derrick logged into the nearest computer, inserted his flash drive, and clicked to print his paper. The system beeped and informed him he could pick up his paper at the librarian station for a twelve-cent per page fee. Derrick exited the screen, ejected his drive, and headed to the librarian's counter.

"Good morning, Miss Betsy," Derrick said.

"Good morning. How may I help you?"

"I printed a document. It should be under Derrick Anders."

Miss Betsy excused herself to the office and returned with Derrick's paper. "Eight pages, that'll be ninety-six cents."

Derrick gave her a dollar and refused the change.

"Do you mind if I ask if that's for Professor Adkins?" Miss Betsy asked, biting the corner of her lip.

"Yes, for his Parent-Child Relationship Course," Derrick replied. "You know him?"

"I've taken his course," she said with a smile.

"Really? Did you have as much difficulty writing for him as I am?" Derrick tried to laugh in jest but didn't succeed.

"He's not the easiest professor to sit under, but he sure is inspirational," she said. "He has been through a lot, so he knows what he's teaching. It's not just book knowledge to him."

"Is that right?" Derrick had difficulty putting other people in situations that compared to his own. It wasn't that he felt they were better than him; it was that he was too focused on getting through his hardship to consider that someone else may have their own struggles.

"I don't want to say too much, but pay attention. He'll give you glimpses into what he's been through. It's when you see those flashes that you begin to learn—not only the subject he's teaching but also about who he is as a person. He may not fully understand it himself, but it's part of what he's here to teach and what I learned under him. So, pay attention, and…" Miss Betsy pulled back with gritted teeth and furrowed brows, "cut him a little slack?"

Derrick smiled, understanding her meaning. "I'll do that. Thanks, Miss Betsy. I appreciate your concern."

Miss Betsy pushed up her glasses and smiled. "Now go, you're going to be late. And you don't want to get bumped a percentage point on my account."

"It's two now," Derrick laughed and obeyed the command, heading out of the library and up the stairs to Professor Adkins's room. He would now look at Professor Adkins through a new pair of eyes, wondering what lurked in his past. Was it like his, a half parentage? He was determined to find out. When he entered the room, Professor Adkins was copying from his Notepad onto the board. Derrick approached the desk and dropped his paper into his 'In' box, where assignments were expected to go. Derrick stood watching him write the next topic of study. He must've felt Derrick's eyes on him because he stopped writing and turned toward him.

"Can I help you, son?"

"Derrick. Derrick Anders."

"Can I help you, Derrick, Derrick Anders?"

"No, sir. I'm just submitting my midterm," Derrick said, not sure what to do next.

"And you've done so, Derrick, Derrick Anders. You may have a seat."

"Oh, right," Derrick said. A couple of students sitting in the front row snickered as he passed.

Way to go, Anders, Derrick said to himself. He took his seat, sulked into it, and hid for the remainder of the period.

After slipping out, he found his next course, Human Development and Family Studies, to be a breeze. Their midterm was a lecture-based Q and A from a local professional in the field. If you answered your question, you passed, if you tripped over your answer, you were given a mediocre grade, and if you couldn't answer, you had some serious makeup work to do. Professor Jaxon didn't fail students, but she did require them to work twice as hard to get a passing grade.

Derrick's question was on the parental role in career choices. Derrick's studies had taken him through case studies on situations much like his own, single-parent homes. But he wasn't ignorant enough to stop there. He gave statistics on the success of dual-parent homes and homes where neither parent was present.

"Fifty-nine percent of widowed parent homes have had students go on to secondary educations; twenty-seven percent of those have gone on to earn their four-year college degree," Derrick explained, then concluded, "I'm hoping to inch that percentage up a notch, Mrs. Jaxon."

"Very well presented, Mr. Anders, Bravo." Mrs. Jaxon applauded.

Derrick sat, heart-pounding, glad that his moment in the spotlight was over, relieved that his question was simple and up his alley. Not saying that his life was a statistic. In fact, he felt he was the exception to the rule. He would laugh whenever he read about how people in his situation were less likely to succeed because they had no support system.

If anything, his mom taught him to carry on despite having no real means of support. Self-sufficiency was one of the main tools in her arsenal. It was now in his. But if professors graded by the percentage sign, he would reluctantly give it.

Professor Jaxon's praise was short-lived as she moved on to her next victim. Her question was not as kind as she was asked about the economics of living today versus living during her parents' age. Obviously, she was ill-prepared, and her stumbling speech lacked the 'percentage signs.' Several students were raising their hands, begging to bail her out, but they nor the student would receive any such luck; this was her midterm. After two minutes of agony, the Professor raised her hand and motioned for her to sit, which she did, her question barely half-answered.

"Mr. Anders, would you care to fill the class in on the details your colleague has left out?"

Why she called on him when half the class had their hands raised was beyond him. Perhaps it was a carry-over from the *very well presented, Mr. Anders* being fresh on her mind. Derrick stood and prepared to give an answer that was going to be quite different than what his colleague would provide— she was female and Hispanic. But he knew his professor was always looking for personal application in student's answers. With that in mind, he threw out her answer and began fresh. Two minutes later, he had another *well done* and an annoyed look from the student who was shunned.

It's not my problem. I studied, Derrick thought as he sat. Instead of sulking back in a chair, Derrick held his head a bit higher. He felt confidence in himself and the pride that his mom had instilled in him. He just wished she were alive today to see it.

"Hey Derrick, before you leave today, we need to detail clean behind the counter. Corporate is coming through, and our location up in Katy received low scores for their front-of-store area," Mr. Lauder explained. "Get with Brian and Breonna. Have them call customers on their holds and get anything that doesn't belong there back on the shelves or to where it belongs."

"Yes, sir," Derrick said, loading up his cart with a stack of returns. He wheeled out onto the sales floor and into the traffic of customers. There was more than the average amount of preschool-aged kids and parents in the store—there must have been a children's release that day. He looked over the books in his cart. To his relief, he didn't see anything that would have him drive that direction.

Derrick finished his first rack without running over any children and without seeing Breonna, now that he thought about it. The boss must have her on a project to suit the suits. He peeked around each corner of non-fiction but didn't see her. His cart was empty, so he would look like a fool just wheeling it around the section, and it would give fodder to those who had been eating up the gossip that she had a thing for him. For him to be seen lingering in her area would only fan the flame of conversation. He adjusted his course and headed back to the registers.

But it was too late.

"Find anything interesting, Der?" Brian asked with a Cheshire Cat grin.

Oh brother, Derrick rolled his eyes and didn't say anything. He went back to the stack of books that was on the counter.

They were dusty from being underneath the counter. Most of them were holds that customers either took their time with or had completely forgotten about. A couple of them looked as if they had been there for months. One of them was old with a faded green cover and gold lettering. He brushed off the dust and froze once he realized what he held in his hands. It was *Angel's Among Us* by Elanor Strong.

Derrick could only stare at his find, and his hand must've gone limp because the next thing he knew, the book had fallen to the ground. The clunk echoed in the small cashier area. It startled Brian, who had been straightening the outside area of the registers.

"Hey!" he shouted.

"Sorry," Derrick apologized and bent over to pick up the book. As he stood and dusted off the spine, he noticed something on the ground. It must've fallen out of the book; it was an old photograph. Derrick picked up the picture. It was a man in his twenties. He was holding a baby and had a huge, proud smile on his face.

He didn't notice Breonna had sidled up to him, "Who's that?" she asked.

Derrick swallowed hard. "I think I'm looking at my father and me."

Chapter
Five

Derrick was never as anxious to finish classes as he was Friday morning. For once in a long time, he had a Friday off. He was going to make the most of it and head to the Downtown Library. There was a man there who could have answers to how a book they were searching for suddenly turned up. He had already asked others in the store about the book just in case someone had found it in the back or had it on order. No one else claimed it.

The first thing Derrick learned was that Houston had a dozen downtown libraries. But there were only two with the Houston Library moniker. The man didn't say Central, but he did say *best*. So, taking the chance, he drove into Downtown Houston in search of the tweed-coated man.

It being a Friday and just past the lunch hour, lawyers, clerks, and other office staff were out and about the city. The streets were packed with vehicles and pedestrians. Derrick found his way through them to the parking area, paid the toll, and pulled into a slot. Leaving his car, he didn't forget the reason for his visit, the copy of *Angels Among Us*.

As Derrick made his way around and up the stairs to the entrance, the other end of society greeted him; the homeless were in more than one area of the courtyard. It was more than he had expected, and his heart went out to them. His pace slowed as he walked toward the entrance. Derrick looked at each vagrant, wondering their story. Was it misfortune? Was it their own doing? Could one event change their plight, as it had for him?

"Spare any change, sir?" One of the ladies took notice of his noticing them and took advantage of his prolonged eye contact. Derrick apologized that he had none. Which was true—he only carried his bank cards. The disheartened woman smiled, "That's okay. You have a good day, sir."

Derrick picked up his pace to avoid further confrontations. He locked his eyes on the front door of the tall building and beelined to and through the entrance.

The lobby of the building was large and open, with each floor visible above. A banner ran across the second-floor tier and read, **Adventure Is In Here!** but with the absence of books, Derrick couldn't tell he was in a library just yet. A bank of elevators was ahead of him, and he could see the library's lower entrance to his left. To his right was a decorated reading area. Tables and chairs, loungers, and sofas were spread throughout. They overlooked a courtyard of trees, and the rest of the city scurrying by.

Near the elevator doors was the library's directory. He fingered down the board and found Religion and Spirituality. It was up a floor and to the right. Derrick punched the elevator button, and it binged. The doors opened, letting a group of excited toddlers off with their exhausted mothers in tow, each with a small stack of must-reads. Derrick wondered if this was the other end of the crowd from the sale at the bookstore. *Those who don't purchase, check out*, he mused. Derrick entered the elevator and punched the second floor.

The elevator binged and opened to his floor. The light from the open floorplan made Derrick shield his eyes for a moment. When they adjusted, he was impressed with the view. He had overheard that this was a recent remodel. The courtyard below was beautiful, although he could see several of the vagrants he had passed coming in, the grounds were well-tended. Perhaps the beauty was part of the reason they were attracted to it. It gave them some sense of peace in their lives.

Derrick looked up at the directory board, Religion and Spirituality would be to his left. All he needed to do now was search for a tweed hat and coat. *Shouldn't be too hard. That is if he still even wore it. It was in the upper seventies. Who would be wearing such a heavy coat on a day like today?* The collar-length white hair would be the next clue. So far, nothing but college-age and a couple of suits passed him as he conducted his search. Derrick was running out of aisles when he heard a familiar voice.

"I see you've made a discovery, Derrick," the older voice called to him.

Derrick turned to see the familiar tweed coat and hat had not changed. It was the man he was searching for. "Yes sir, I found the book. It has an amazing story."

"Oh, I do love a good story," the man began to glow. He stepped toward Derrick. "We all have a story to tell, Derrick. Happy stories, sad stories, true stories, made-up stories, anything and everything. Life isn't life without a good story. I have a story. You have a story. It's what makes us who we are. And we need to tell people about our stories. Without telling our stories," the man gestured to the bookshelf beside him, "we're just books sitting on a shelf."

"And do I have a story to tell you…" Derrick paused.

"I'm sorry, where are my manners. The name is Carter. Carter Jennings," he said as he extended his hand.

Derrick shook it and returned the greeting. "Can we sit down? I'd like to talk to you."

"Certainly," Carter began. "Say, are you hungry? There is a sandwich shop not too far from here. Davies Deli. They serve a great sandwich. And it's Friday. They have a Reuben you need to try. Too bad it's not Monday though, their meatloaf sandwich is spectacular."

"Maybe some other time. I really need to talk to you about this book."

"Certainly, certainly. Let's sit over here. We'll have a bit more privacy," Carter said, leading him to a back reading area.

Derrick held on tight to the book. He was having second thoughts about letting it go. With the photo inside, chances are this was the book his mom read to him when he was little. He was still not sure how it ended up in his store, but it did, and now he was in possession of a memory, and the man in front of him may have an answer.

"Did you have trouble finding the library?"

"Not at all. Streets were a bit busy with the lunch hour, but I made it all right."

"Wonderful. The improvements they have made here are spectacular. I've been away for a few years; it wasn't like this when I left."

"Where have you been?"

"Here and there. I was in Salt Lake City before returning.

Monday, in fact. No offense to the Beehive State, but I just love Texas. I was glad to get back. Maybe that meatloaf sandwich had something to do with it?"

Derrick had to laugh. "They really have a meatloaf sandwich? I've never heard of such a thing."

"That's what makes Darren and Angela Davies restaurant geniuses," Carter said. "The family calls him *Pop*. He created a sandwich for every day of the week based on family favorites. Meatloaf, Caesar Salad, and a Supreme Pizza. You name it, he most likely has a sandwich for it."

"That sounds amazing," Derrick said. "We'll have to make our way over there one day."

"It's a date," Carter said, slapping his knee. "Well, enough about food. I know you want to talk about the book in your hand.

"Yes, I do," Derrick began. He grabbed the edges of the book and just stared at it as he began to speak. "You already know that *Angels Among Us* was the book that Mom used to read to me when I was little. What you don't know is that my mom passed away not too long ago. Three years ago, in fact. When she passed, my copy of this book disappeared. So did many other items.

"It was my aunt. She went through my mother's belongings sold many of them. I didn't really know her reasoning. Maybe she was trying to protect me from having to do it. I was only eighteen at the time, and I guess I wouldn't know what to do with an adult woman's clothing and personal effects. But among some of the things that disappeared were some things that I would have preferred to keep.

"My aunt stayed around Sunnyside for about a year, then she moved away not too long after I graduated high school.

Since I had a decent job and my scholarships and grants were helping fund my schooling, she didn't bother checking in on me. Now I work to pay the bills and what's left of Mom's mortgage, which is a whole other story. As for the book, I hadn't thought about it until you came in yesterday." Derrick looked up at Carter. His grey eyes were locked on every word, he had a knowing look, but it was more. Derrick would almost call it stunned.

"What?" Derrick asked. "What's wrong?"

"Who are you?" Carter asked, then sat up. "What is your name?"

"What? You know my name. Derrick Anders."

"Your full name?" Carter said with an edge to his tone.

"Derrick Anders. I don't have a middle name," Derrick said, a little nervous at Carter's sudden irritability.

"Who was your mother?"

"Angela Robertson," Derrick said.

Carter stared at Derrick, his face frozen in shock. He began to look over every feature: his eyes, nose, and ears.

Derrick began to feel he was being peeled back layer by layer.

Derrick couldn't take the silence any longer. "You knew my mom, didn't you," Derrick asked. Carter's expression revealed he had struck a nerve.

"Are you Ricky?" Carter asked, eyebrow raised.

When Carter said 'Ricky' a thousand images flashed through Derrick's: The boy who had done the dishes because Mom worked a late shift, the child who had helped his mom study to pass her MCATS so she could become a nurse, the teen who sat on the stairs and heard her talking to the man in the hat.

The man in the hat. The man in the *tweed* hat.

The recognition between the men was instantaneous. The mutual woman they both lost was a burden they shared and a pain they still carried. Derrick blamed the man in the hat for his mom getting sick and dying. The man in the hat blamed himself for losing the soul of the woman with the son named Ricky.

Neither of them was ready for this revelation. Neither of them was prepared for this confrontation.

"I need to go," Carter said. He turned on his heels and headed for the exit.

"Wait," Derrick said. "Carter. You can't just leave. We need to talk about this."

Carter didn't respond, he kept walking. Derrick didn't pursue. What was he going to do if he caught him anyhow? What was he going to say? The tweed coat and hat turned into the elevator and disappeared out of sight.

Derrick looked down at the book and opened it. The photo of his father peeked out at him, and the question suddenly occurred to him. *Did Carter know his father?* Derrick slammed the book closed and ran for the elevator. He pushed the button, but it didn't open. He turned around and looked out into the lobby. The man in the hat, Carter, was near the exit door.

"Carter. Wait! Don't go! Wait!"

Carter didn't turn around.

"Stop! I need to know. Did you know my father? Stop, Carter!" Derrick yelled. If it had not been such a high drop, Derrick would have made the jump. What was he thinking of letting him leave? What would happen now? What if he never saw him again?

The elevator binged, and Derrick spun and entered it,

pushing the button a dozen times to let the elevator know he meant business. The doors started to close but quickly flung open as a late arrival had reached their arm in to beat the device. Derrick sighed. Now it was no use. Carter would be gone for sure. The crowd, bus, or cab; he was a memory.

The doors opened on the lower level, and Derrick walked to the front desk.

"Can I help you, sir?"

"Yes. There's a gentleman who frequents here. His name is Carter. He wears a tweed coat and hat. Do you know who I'm talking about?"

"Carter? White hair and tan coat?"

"Yeah."

"Oh yes. I think I know who you're talking about. Didn't know his name, but I've seen a man come in who looks like that the past few days."

"So, he comes in here a lot then?"

"I'm not sure. I've just seen him the last day or two. But we've just reopened from a remodel, so I can't tell you how regular folks have visited. It's difficult to tell."

"Thank you. I understand. He's been here the last couple of days, though?"

"I believe so," the worker said.

Derrick sighed. "Okay, thanks." He turned to the exit and back out to his car, passing the vagabonds on his way out.

Derrick had no idea where to begin searching for Carter. He thought back to their first meeting at the bookstore. Did Carter know something he didn't back then? It almost felt like Carter was searching for him now. But why all of a sudden was his search disrupted? Why did the revelation of who his mom was make a difference? Who was this *Carter*?

Then something Carter had said suddenly made Derrick famished. After Googling *Davies Deli*, he found that they closed at 5 PM; it was a little after 4:00. Clearly not enough time to get there, sit, eat, and find out what he needed to know about Carter. Anxious as he was, tomorrow was another day. With no school and a late shift, he would be having lunch at a new diner. Sandwiches with a theme—who knew? He was, in a way, excited about what Davies may have on the menu tomorrow and what answers they may have about who Carter may be.

Chapter
Six

"This can't be it," Derrick told himself as he pulled up to the brown, two-toned Hardie-siding double wide. If there weren't so many cars in front of it, he would've thought he was lost. A large painted sign that read:

Davies Deli: Home of the Meatloaf Sandwich

was affixed to the roof. *Okay, this is definitely the place.*

Derrick parked his car and walked up the steps and into the dining area. He was blown away by what he saw. It was like stepping into the '60s. There was a counter at the front with circular stools, a checkered tile floor and counter backsplash, and a well-stocked dessert case at the end of the stools. Booths lined the walls to his right and wrapped around the far wall—nearly all were full. He looked back to the counter, only a couple of spots were open—one near the register and one near a guy on his computer sitting beside the dessert case.

Derrick chose the latter. It appeared the servers were using the first space as a resting spot as there were a few unattended drinks. He could see them buzzing around with trays of baskets filled with the most delicious smells. While it wasn't meatloaf, he was sure it would be an interesting experience to try. He sat and briefly glanced at the screen of his neighbor. He recognized the writing program as the one he used for his documents. The guy with the computer stared back at him.

"Sorry, I don't mean to intrude. Great writing program. I use it to write my term papers for school," Derrick said.

"I love it," the man said. "I've used it for years. Since I was in school myself."

The server walked up, interrupting them. "Hey sweetie, I'm Jasmine. What can I get you to drink?"

"Sweet tea would be great, thanks."

"Have you looked over the menu yet? Or would you like to know about the special?"

The man spoke up, "You've got to try the Reuben. It's the best in the county."

"Sorry, sir. I don't particularly care for kraut."

The man stuck out his bottom lip. "Well, then we may have to ask you to leave. We don't take kindly to that type of negativity around here."

The waitress laughed. "Aaron, knock it off. Leave the poor man alone. It's obviously his first time here."

Derrick smiled. "I just wish it were Monday. I've heard some good things about the meatloaf sandwich."

"Didya now," Aaron said with a chuckle. He turned to Jasmine and smiled. "Go back and ask Pop to whip up a meatloaf special for my friend here. But keep it on the down-low. Don't want folks to be swarming around." Aaron looked up at Jasmine and smiled, then back to Derrick with a wink.

"Right-o, boss," Jasmine said and headed into the kitchen.

"Boss?" Derrick said. "I thought Darren and Angela Davies owned this place?"

Aaron looked around. "Yeah, they do. Well, in a way, did. Mom passed away about six months ago. Pop's still around, but he didn't want to continue the deli alone. He asked me to partner with him to run it. So, when I'm not writing for *The Chronicle*," Aaron gestured to his computer, then to the kitchen, "I'm here helping Pop with the deli."

"So, *Mom* and *Pop*? They're your parents?"

"Not exactly. I was involved with their daughter before she passed. I became more or less their surrogate. They wouldn't have it any other way than for me to call them that."

"I'm so sorry, Aaron. I lost a family member myself a few years ago—my mother. It's kinda what brings me here today."

"How so?" Aaron asked as Jasmine placed a meatloaf sandwich in front of him and refilled their teas.

"Do you happen to know who Carter Jennings is?"

Aaron choked on the tea he had just sipped. It took him several seconds to regain his composure. He held out his finger to tell Derrick and a concerned Jasmine that he would be fine. Aaron took a deep breath and released it.

"Did you say, Carter Jennings?"

"Yeah, why? Who is Carter Jennings?"

"It's difficult to explain, Derrick. But you came to the right place. I think God has sent you here for a reason. You do believe in God, right?"

Derrick's face went pale. He wasn't sure how to answer that question. He didn't want to sound ignorant or rude, but he didn't want to lie either. "I'm not sure what to say to that, Aaron. My mom told me that God always had His hand on us. And I do remember going to church from time to time. I had my Sunday School teacher as my babysitter for most of my life. I also understand that I couldn't be where I am today without some sort of divine help. So, do I believe there is a God? Most definitely. Am I active in that belief today? No, I'm not."

"I appreciate your honesty, Derrick. It's comforting, and the fact that you do believe in God is half the struggle. But the other factor is that you have Carter Jennings looking after you. This should tell you so much more. But I can't tell you what that is. That's what you need to figure out on your own."

"What's that supposed to mean," Derrick said, both confused and annoyed.

"Please, don't be upset. It just means that God has a purpose for Carter's involvement in your life. He will work it out, and all of this will be revealed in God's time."

"How do you know that?"

"Let's just say that you aren't the only one who's had their life impacted by Carter Jennings," Aaron said, placing his hand on Derrick's shoulder. "And I don't mean that in a negative way, either. Be patient and hear him out."

"That may be a problem," Derrick said, pulling the book out of the bag he was carrying and handing it to Aaron. "I don't know if this book means anything to you, but it meant something to Carter and to me. It's what set him storming off."

"What do you mean, storming off?"

"I work at a bookstore. Carter came in claiming he was looking for a book, *Angels Among Us*. We didn't have it. I told him about my mom reading it to me as a child. Oddly enough, the next day, as I was cleaning the store, that book mysteriously showed up. Actually, I think that book *is* my mother's copy. I just don't know how it got into my store."

"Carter," Aaron said, matter-of-factly.

"That's what I figured," Derrick said, pointing to the book.

"The book didn't appear until the day after Carter came into the store, and it's odd that it's the same book he was asking about. Too odd to be a coincidence."

"Don't be freaked out by it, Derrick. There *is* a purpose behind all of it. God has a purpose, and all will be revealed in due time. Just be patient."

"There's more," Derrick said. He handed Aaron the photo of him and his dad. "That's a photograph of what I believe to be my father and me. I never knew him because he supposedly died not too long after that picture was taken."

"How did he die?"

"I was never told. I never had the guts to ask my mom before she passed away. She never really spoke of him. The only thing I ever received from him was his last name. Even she didn't keep that from her marriage. She went back to using her maiden name. It was one of the things that upset Carter when we spoke that day."

"Let's go back to that. You've mentioned that twice already. What do you mean by *Carter was upset*? I've never known him to be upset."

"Well, the man I saw yesterday was upset. When I first met him, he was kind, and I would go as far as saying he was loving. But when we got on the subject of who I was and who my mom was, he became upset and stormed off. Things were going so well; I don't know what went wrong."

"You said you were talking about who you and your mom are. What upset him about that?"

"When he asked for my mom's name, he became upset. Then he asked me about a pet name that only my mom called me; Rick. I don't know how he could have known that name. But then I remembered something." The thoughts came back to Derrick again, the memories of that night on the stairwell landing and the man in the hat. He recalled the man's voice talking to his mom. While he couldn't make out what they were saying, he knew his mom was upset at what she was hearing. *What could Carter have been telling her that would hurt her so much?*

"It was a little more than three years ago," Derrick continued. "I knew she was upset. I don't know why I didn't go down to her. I was turning eighteen the following week. I could've handled the situation. I don't know what happened with them. I never saw or heard from the man again. My mom died three months later."

"Are you're confident it was Carter?" Aaron asked.

"I am now. Now that I've thought it through, I don't know why I didn't realize it sooner. It's the hat that gives him away. That same tweed hat."

Aaron chuckled. "I'm sorry. I apologize. Is he still wearing that worn brown tweed coat and hat?"

"Yeah, I suppose. I've only seen him a couple of times."

"Again, I'm sorry. Continue."

"I just wish I knew what he wanted from me and what set him off."

"He'll turn up again. Trust me. He's not going anywhere. He has a job to do and will complete it as he's been instructed."

"Sorry I keep asking this, but what does that mean?"

"Just trust me. I can't say more than what you need to know right now. All will be revealed to you when the timing is right. Just be patient. Go about your life, and it would help if you did become more active in your faith. It did for me."

"So, you've been visited by Carter Jennings?"

"You can say that," Aaron admitted. Which was half-true;

Deborah was the true recipient of Carter's visitation. He was just a witness to the miracle of God through that visitation. Plus, he did have his own encounter and a revelation of how Deborah's life and Carter's visitation impacted his own life.

"If you see Carter again, let him know I'm looking for him. I'd like to clarify a few things," Derrick said, picking up his sandwich. "Now I'm about to tear into this sandwich that everyone seems so awestruck over."

Aaron smiled. "It will change your life."

Derrick took his first bite, and he was sold. Pop's meatloaf sandwich was as advertised. No, it was even better. There were no words to describe what he was eating. He almost forgot the reason he had come into the establishment. He and Aaron talked shop for a bit; writing programs and his plans for the next year and a half. Aaron mentioned that they had a waitress who attended UH a few years ago, Derrick seemed to recollect an Ericka, a senior, while he was a wet behind the ears freshman, but he wasn't entirely sure. Ericka was now a nurse for one of the major health systems.

Derrick left the deli with the agreement that he would be back. He wanted more information on who Carter Jennings was, why he was so interested in who he was, and why it was so hush-hush. Aaron instructed him to go about his life and that time would show him that God would reveal everything in due time. Derrick couldn't help but wonder what God and Carter Jennings had to do with each other.

Chapter
Seven

Derrick worked through his shift with one eye on the customers and the other on the front door looking for Carter. He didn't expect him to come to the store, but he didn't want to miss him if he did. When he asked Brian to be on the lookout for a white-haired man in a tweed coat, he looked at him like he was insane, so he left off asking anyone else to watch for him. His saving grace was that Brian had been there and *sorta remembered* seeing the customer. After his short shift, with no sign of Carter, Derrick went home and raided his refrigerator of leftover meatloaf sandwich and fries, then called it a night.

The following morning was brisk from a front that had blown through; Fall was in full effect. It being Sunday, there would be no tacos. Maria's was closed. However, there was sure to be doughnuts and coffee in the Fellowship Hall of Faith Community. The church was just a few blocks away, so Derrick chose to walk. It brought back memories of how he and his mom made their way to church. She always said it gave them the opportunity to prepare their hearts.

Derrick was not quite sure of the reception he would receive or if the same people would be there, but he was confident Sister Georgia would greet him with a hug and a kiss on each cheek—that is, if she could reach him. He hadn't seen her since the funeral three years ago. Since then, other folks from the church checked on him now and then, but he supposed his aunt made it clear they were not welcome, because they slowly stopped coming around. He would occasionally run into one of them at the grocery store or at the gas station where they'd exchange pleasantries, but that was it. He left it alone because religion was more of his mom's thing than his anyway.

He rounded the corner and saw the bright white church in the center of the block. The street was already lined with cars, which meant that the lot was already full. Derrick looked at his watch, and it was still early. He crossed the street and saw a couple of men in suits standing in front of the doors. One was helping an elderly lady in a bright yellow dress up the steps to the door. He followed the sidewalk along a wrought iron gate toward the entrance. He passed a tall wooden cross that reached into the sky and the marquee announcing the services for the week.

At the steps, one of the men greeted him with an extended hand. "Good morning, sir. How are you today? Welcome to Faith Community."

Derreck accepted the handshake. "Thank you. It's my first time in a long time. I used to come here with my mom a few years ago."

"Wonderful to have you back, sir."

"Derrick."

"Wonderful to have you back, Derrick," the man corrected

himself. "I'm sorry, I don't know you. I'm fairly new here. Just been attending for a couple of months. I'm sure there are many inside who will be excited to see you."

"I'm a bit nervous about just that," Derrick said.

"No, brother. Don't be concerned about that. We're all God's children. We have our reasons for being away, and we have reasons for coming home. You will be well received," the man nodded his head toward the entrance. "I'm Terrance. You need anything, find me."

"Thank you, Terrance. I'll do that," Derrick shook his hand again and looked at the door. He took a slow step toward it, then another. The next thing he knew, he was inside. The sounds of conversations, children's laughter, and piano music wrapped around him. He looked at faces in the crowd and tried to place anyone but came up empty. It had been three years, and as a teenager, he wasn't one to record anyone's face or name into long-term storage. As for him, he was fifty pounds heavier and had a face full of hair. He was virutally unrecognizable, the invisable man. The only one who would possibly see through his physical change would be—

"Derrick, Derrick Anders? Is that you?!" came a familiar voice from his left. Derrick turned to see a beautifully bonneted Sister Georgia.

"Yes, Sister Georgia, it's me." Derrick had to smile. Her familiarity gave him the comfort he was seeking. "How are you this morning?"

"I'm doing much better seeing you in God's house. I've been praying for this day," she said, giving him a once over. "Goodness, you have grown."

Derrick laughed.

"Louise. Roberta. Come over here and meet Derrick. He's

Angela Robertson's boy. Well, I guess you're more of a man today. How old are you now?"

"Twenty-one. I'm a student over at the university."

"Fabulous. Your mama would be proud," Sister Georgia said.

"She's part of why I'm doing it."

"Well, good. I'm proud of you," she said. Sister Georgia introduced him to many of her friends that morning. Many remembered the boy who would peek over the pew or ask the silly questions in Sunday School. Some sparked a memory, others not so much, for which he felt guilty.

The piano built to a crescendo announcing it was time for the congregants to take their seats, and the service was about to begin. Sister Georgia grabbed his arm, directing him to sit with her. He was glad she wasn't a front pew sitter. He was not prepared to be front and center to draw the pastor's attention. But with the church as packed as it was, it was unlikely he would be noticed anyhow.

He hadn't been to church in a long time and wasn't sure what to expect. He wasn't sure if the pastor would come out, shouting, or the choir would be howling out worship songs. They appeared fairly somber at the moment. Twelve men and women in gowns were now swaying and clapping along with the piano. He didn't recognize the tune, not that he expected to remember any of the music he had heard as a kid.

The choir began to hum along with the piano's tune, clapping to the beat. They continued for a couple of measures. The melodies and harmonies were in perfect pitch. One of the choir members stepped up to the microphone and began to sing the words to the tune. The hook of the song rang, "To God be the glory, great things he has done." A chorus of *Amens* echoed from the congregation as the soloist sang the words. Some people around him raised their hands, and others swayed along with the choir. Derrick watched in amazement at everyone's involvement in the ceremony.

The musical experience finished, and the choir sat. A man who sat in the front row stood and approached the podium on the stage. *The pastor, perhaps?* Derrick mused.

"Good morning, congregation. I have just a few announcements before we begin our service this morning, and Pastor delivers the message…" the portly fellow began. He went on to talk about mid-week services, a soup kitchen that was looking for donations and volunteers, and a reminder that the holiday season was approaching and to remember the less fortunate. He closed with prayer and turned the service over to another gentleman introduced as Brother Michael.

"Thank you, Brother. I'm excited for today. I have been praying through the music, and I know God has led you here this morning. I trust God will lead us into His presence as we lift up His Holy Name through song," Brother Michael set aside his microphone and turned to the choir. He looked over to the pianist, and she began to play. Sister Georgia handed him a hymnal to follow along as Brother Michael called out the page number of the hymn. As with the first song, the choir was angelic and even had him moving and clapping along at times. After the final song, they were closed in prayer and asked to be seated.

Derrick wasn't sure what to expect from the pastor. He was doing what Aaron had suggested, *becoming more active in his belief*, hoping for answers. If God was trying to tell him something, and God used pastors as his spokespeople, then this would be the opportune time to get through to him—God had a captive audience.

"Sometimes," the pastor began, "those who appear to need the least amount of help, are the very ones who need it the most." He paused and took in the room. It was silent. He scanned to the back aisle of the congregation, then up to the front on Derrick's side. He locked eyes with Derrick for a moment. Derrick wasn't sure if it was because he was new or to make a point. The pastor looked back down at his Bible on the podium and continued his sermon.

Thirty minutes later, there was no lightning bolt from heaven. Derrick wasn't convinced the pastor had the answers he was seeking. He felt comfortable with his situation. He was confident in his success with schooling. And other than the mishap with Carter and misunderstanding his intentions with the book, he felt comfortable where his life was headed. He didn't think he needed the help the pastor was speaking of. He figured God was already on his side. His mom had prayed for it every night.

On his way back home, he pondered his situation. He hoped he hadn't let Aaron down. He had tried the church, but maybe it just wasn't for him. He enjoyed the music and felt it was beautiful and powerful, but God wasn't the center of his life the way He seemed to be for them. Yes, he believed in God, just not at the same level as the people in that building. Not the way Breonna seemed to live. If she knew how he felt, he wondered if she would still be interested in him. From what he understood, Christians being involved with non-Christians was a kind of a deal-breaker.

Derrick started to wonder what it would be like at Breonna's church. Did she attend a Baptist church like his? What about Aaron? It would be interesting to experience another denomination to see how they expressed their worship. It was comparable to what he was learning through his studies. As a social worker, he had to learn about different cultures to relate to the people he encountered—no two are alike. That seemed especially true when it came to religion. It was one of the scariest topics. His mom knew what she believed and was never afraid to express it. It was probably why it was so ingrained in him to believe *in* God. He was confident in his belief in a God, but just not to the level of committing to Him.

Chapter
Eight

Derrick had little luck tracking down Carter early in the week. It was now Wednesday, and he was on his way to work. Midterm grades were supposed to be posted that day but hadn't been posted by the time he left campus. Not that it mattered. He didn't have time to check if they *had* been posted. He sprinted down the stairs, this time a freshman-free hall, and there wasn't a drop of rain on his drive through the park. He still had twenty minutes to get to work, so he was confident he would clock in on time for once. The only thing that would keep him from getting to work on time would be a man in a tweed hat. *Much like the man sitting on the bench in the park over there,* Derrick thought.

Derrick slammed on his brakes. So did the car behind him, almost ending up in his backseat. Even through the closed windows, he could hear the expletives hurled at him. Derrick squinted his eyes, and on a park bench along the trail sat the man—wearing a tweed coat and hat, just like Carter Jennings. It was a decent distance, so he couldn't be 100% sure, but sure enough to impede traffic. Derrick looked ahead and saw a parking lot about a hundred yards off. He pulled into it and found a spot.

There was a walking path that circled the park and met up with the lot. Derrick followed the path to where he believed he had seen Carter. A couple with their spaniel occupied the first bench, the second was empty, and the third was further down than he figured Carter had been. That bench housed a power walker stretching her legs. Derrick went back to the couple with the spaniel.

"Excuse me," Derrick said. "You didn't happen to see an older gentleman in a dark brown coat and hat sitting on the bench over there, did you?"

The spaniel spun around Derrick's legs, wagging its tail, he barked once. Derrick wasn't sure if that was an answer or just a playful pet. He bent over and scratched the pet behind its ears.

"I'm sorry, no, we haven't paid too much attention to anyone who has walked by," the man of the group said. "We've been trying to keep our eye on our little one. The last time we were here, he got off his leash, and we had a hard time getting him back on it. When we tried to catch him, he thought we were playing."

"You should ask *the runner*," said the female, with a bit of agitation in her voice. She pointed to the girl who was still stretching two benches down.

"Oh, come on, Emm, I wasn't looking at her. It's all in your head," the man said, extending his hand out, pleading his case. A bomb could have exploded in the park, and they wouldn't have seen it. Derrick thought it was best to make his exit. He thanked both of them, which neither heard amidst their growing argument, and left.

He looked down toward the sprinter but thought better of approaching her. He wanted answers, but if she were as focused as they had been, she wouldn't have seen Carter either. Plus, someone like him doesn't approach someone like her in the middle of a park and start asking strange questions about a man who appears to be avoiding him. He turned and walked to his car. *He must've heard the breaks and saw my car.* Derrick thought. *I spooked him. I lost him again. But at least I have another location to add to my list of places to look for him.*

Derrick's radio clock informed him he was now five minutes late for work. His palm slammed into the steering wheel, and he put his car into drive. That same clock read fifteen minutes late when he shut off the engine in the parking lot. He thought of sprinting to the time clock. But 270 pounds doesn't sprint, and the ramification of that sprint was less welcome than the chewing he was about to receive. He would walk the lot to the building. It was the corporation's policy for them to park this far anyhow. Many associates felt they should be paid from the time they parked; it took so long.

Mocha and the A/C wafted over Derrick's senses as the doors opened, while Brian's shame-on-you finger sweep mocked him yet again. Derrick smirked and nodded in agreement. He turned his eyes to the carpeted floor and dragged his tucked tail to the backroom to clock in.

He barely made it through periodicals when a familiar, bright, and unexpected voice called to him.

"Hey Derrick. How are you?"

Derrick raised his head, and the cloud that hung over him was dispelled by the ray of sunshine that was Breonna Greene's smile. "Hey, Breonna. What are you doing here? Isn't it a church night for you?"

Breonna frowned. "Yes, but Mr. Lauder called and said that both Simon and Angela called out. He practically begged me to come in. I figured helping people is what God wants us to do. How can I share that with others then shun them when they ask for my help? How Christian is that?"

Derrick nodded. "True. I suppose it would be like a singer who constantly took lessons, but never performed their own show."

Breonna smirked. "Yeah, I suppose. I don't really compare it to performing, but I see your point."

Derrick looked over his shoulder and could see Mr. Lauder walking their way. "Dangit. I'll talk to you later, Breonna. I need to clock in."

"Oh, your late?"

Derrick shook his head and walked toward the back doors, "Yeah, it seems to be my signature. If I'm not back out in fifteen, send a search party, will ya?"

"Um, yeah, sure. Sorry," she called after him as the swinging doors swooshed shut behind him.

Derrick could hear the mumbled conversation between Mr. Lauder and Breonna as he swiped his badge. He walked toward Mr. Lauder's office, prepared for the scolding he was about to receive. He heard the swoosh, and turned and faced his boss.

"Good evening, Mr. Anders. Heh, it seems the tardy bug can be catching," he began.

"Yes, sir. I'm sorry."

"Sorry? What for? You don't need to apologize. I'm the one who is late. It's my own fault. I guess I can see where you come from having other obligations so close to your start time. We'll talk later about bumping your start time a half-hour on Wednesdays. Would that work for you, since it seems your delay is about that?"

Derrick was taken aback—one, because he got away with being late, and two, his boss, known for being inflexible, was now willing to be open regarding his start time. This is what Breonna would call *a blessing*. He was at a loss for words. He hadn't realized Mr. Lauder was waiting for a reply.

"Oh, sorry. Yes, that would help out a lot, Mr. Lauder." Derrick stuck out his hand, Mr. Lauder accepted it. "You have no idea how much it will help."

"As I hope it helped today," Mr. Lauder grinned.

"Excuse me?"

"Today. The reason you were tardy today. The traffic between the school and here can be treacherous."

Derrick's face went pale. *No way. It couldn't have been.* He was so stunned that he failed to notice he hadn't let go of Mr. Lauder's hand.

"I—better get to work, sir," Derrick said, releasing his grip to avoid going into further details.

The night was busy, and he didn't see much of Mr. Lauder after their encounter. He rarely left the register area. His mind was so wrapped up in his near auto claim with his boss that he had forgotten about his midterm grade, that Breonna was somewhere on the sales floor, and that sitting on a park bench somewhere was a man who could have some answers about his father.

Mr. Lauder locked the doors, and the team went to their respective vehicles. All except Breonna. She stood by the doors rubbing her arms in the cold evening. She looked both ways across the parking lot, then exhaled in frustration. She had a forgotten look on her face.

"Everything okay, Breonna?" Derrick asked, already knowing the answer.

"I think my brother forgot about me," she said.

"What happened to your car?"

"He has it. I lent it to him so he could go to church. He just got his license, and he doesn't have his own car. But I'm here, which left him without a ride. So, big sis to the rescue."

"And he forgot what time you got off," Derrick said, trying to soften the blow.

"I certainly hope that's the case."

Derrick looked both ways. No headlights were heading their way. He looked toward car, trying to remember the state of his vehicle, then back to her, "Would you like a ride?"

She repeated his scan, then her eyes met his. "Yeah," she said, her voice soft with a hint of apprehension.

"No problem. I'm the Toyota three miles out," Derrick pointed to his car under the parking lot lamp. It was well lit. Hopefully, that would give her a bit more comfort. "Would you like me to go get it, or do you want to walk with me."

"I'll walk with you. I'm not standing here alone," she said.

"Sorry about your brother," Derrick said.

"It's okay. I'm just glad he chose to go without me. He's struggling with his faith. You know, peer pressure and all."

"He doesn't believe in God?"

"He does, but the kids at school can be mean, especially about Christianity. And Ellis can be impressionable. I wouldn't want him to walk away from faith because of what his friends at school say."

"Kids can be mean. I went through that not having a dad

and trying to be a good student. If you aren't like them, they'll do all they can to bring you down to their level. It's tough to get past it and succeed. But with you by his side, cheering him on, he'll get there. Don't give up."

Derrick could see her smile return in the mix of darkness and lamplight.

"Thank you, Derrick. That means a lot," Breonna said as they reached his car. Derrick walked to her side and unlocked the door. She sat inside, and he closed it behind her, sighing in relief that the seat was trash and fry-free.

Once seated, Derrick started the engine and gave it a rev. "Sorry, she needs to warm up a bit. She's old but runs well. I'll turn the heat on in a sec."

Breonna rubbed her arms, her hands still tucked half into the sleeves. "It's okay. How long have you had it? Sorry—her?"

Derrick laughed. "Since I started driving, seventeen? Four years now. She was in a parking lot graveyard, and a man in our church sold it to me for three hundred. He told me it just needed a bit of TLC and some under the hood work. I Googled most of what needed to be done and repaired it myself. She's purred ever since." As if to prove a point, Derrick revved the engine. Breonna laughed. Derrick looked at the dash, the temp gauge let him know that the heater could be turned on.

"Are you hungry?"

Breonna was silent for a moment, then nodded. "Yeah. I could go for something."

As if scripted, a squeal came from the entrance on their left. A Honda sped up to the bookstore entrance, and stopped at the front door. Breonna growled.

"Let me guess. Ellis?"

"Ellis," she said. She looked at him across the car, her eyes glowing in what little parking lot light was coming into the vehicle. "Some other time?"

"You can count on it," Derrick said. He drove to where Ellis was idling, probably scared out of his wits over an angry sister and the thought of never be allowed to borrow her vehicle again.

As Breonna opened the car door, she dosed him with her patented smile, "Thank you for staying with me, Derrick. I enjoyed our time together."

Derrick laughed. "Even as brief as it was, so did I. See you tomorrow."

They said their good-nights, and Ellis was forced into the passenger seat as Breonna assumed the driving role. Derrick could only imagine the scolding her little brother was receiving, or maybe he couldn't. He couldn't imagine a foul word ever leaving those pretty lips. A pair of lips he wouldn't mind becoming familiar with himself.

Chapter
Nine

"**N**ow I know he's avoiding me, Aaron," Derrick said. "I'm sure he saw me, and when I went over to him, he vanished."

Aaron rubbed his chin with folded arms. "That isn't like Carter. He's the first one to help people. He's the one who seeks and finds, not runs and hides."

"Who is he?"

Aaron was quiet in contemplation. He looked up at the kitchen window at Pop, who was peeking out. He knew about Carter as well. Not only through his brief encounter, but also through the detailed explanations Aaron had given him. But Aaron wasn't sure if giving Derrick this information was a good idea at this point. He still had personal matters to work out before such revelation was made. Usually, *the assignment* as explained to him, was to figure it out as the Reminders were discovered. Aaron wondered how many of them he had discovered so far. Derrick had talked about the book and photo. That was one, but there would be others.

"The book," Aaron began. "You say you found it at your work. And the photo was inside the book?"

Derrick's face contorted, then he nodded. "Yes. I found the book where I work. But I still believe that Carter put it there."

"Right," Aaron said. "I'm not disputing that. Just trying to clarify a couple of things."

"Okay," Derrick nodded and bit his bottom lip.

"Let me ask you this. Have you come across any other interesting finds or occurrences other than the book?"

"No, not that… wait!" Derrick said. His eyes lit up as he remembered something.

"What is it?"

"The headband," Derrick said, pointing to his head. "Breonna has one of my mom's headbands."

"Breonna is the girl you work with?"

"Yes, the one who's interested in me. The one *I'm* interested in. Okay, maybe we're into each other. But that's beside the point. She came into work one day, and she was wearing a headband. It was one that my mother had made. Breonna said she bought it at a rummage sale."

"A rummage sale. How did it get there?"

"When my mom passed, my aunt donated most of my mom's stuff. I was either too upset or young to notice that her knitting was also donated. My mom used to knit headbands, scarves, doilies… she just loved to knit. It was her way of unwinding. I know her style, and when I saw Breonna's headband, I knew it was my mom's work."

"Interesting," Aaron said. "Anything else?"

Derrick's eyes darted then he shook his head. "No, not that I'm aware of. Just those two things."

"Okay," Aaron said. "And you haven't seen or heard anything from Carter since you're meeting at the library?"

"Nothing."

"How long has it been since you found the book?"

"What difference does it make? How is this going to give me answers about where Carter is and how he knows my mother?"

"Just trust me here, Derrick. It's all about the timeline," Aaron said. He could see Derrick was becoming impatient. He needed to give him something soon.

"A week, maybe?"

"A week?" Aaron said, eyebrows raised.

Derrick shrunk back, "Why, what's wrong?"

"Hmm," Aaron said. He didn't remember going a week without some contact from Carter. Even if it was a random hello, he was very much interested in the progress of his assignments. From the impression he received from his encounter, it was his passion.

"What aren't you telling me, Aaron?"

Aaron sighed again. He leaned over and locked eyes with Derrick. "Derrick, I love you brother. I really do. But you *will* understand in due time. Please be patient."

His sincerity must have won him over, because Derrick stopped pushing for information. And he was glad because he already knew Derrick wasn't prepared spiritually for what was coming. That was supposed to come through further Reminders—Reminders that, for some reason, were no longer coming.

Where is Carter? Aaron asked himself.

Derrick finished his Fried Chicken Sandwich and Mom's special sweet tea, and Aaron insisted on comping the meal. After a couple of back and forths, Derrick relented with gratitude. Aaron was glad to hear about Derrick's experience at church. He asked him if he was going back. Derrick shrugged and gave an unreassured "Maybe." Aaron encouraged him to continue going, or if he didn't feel comfortable, he was more than welcome to visit his church. This seemed to appease Derrick. He nodded, smiled, and thanked him. After his basket was empty, he refilled his tea, and the two men said their goodbyes, agreeing to meet sometime during the weekend.

Aaron watched him walk to his vehicle and drive off. He felt for the boy. He just wished he could give him the answers he wanted. He wished he had more answers himself. Aaron looked up at Pop, whose chef hat was again dancing back and forth in the window, still full of life in the kitchen he loved. He picked up his tea, and after a long sip, opened up his laptop and went back to work on his column for the *Journal*.

"We sure are in a pickle, aren't we, Aaron," said a voice behind him.

Aaron turned around, not recognizing the voice. He looked the man over, unable to place him: Blue jeans, plaid shirt, and a Houston ball cap over his shoulder-length blonde hair. The face was solid and serious. The blue eyes locked on his and wouldn't let go.

"Do I know you, sir?" Aaron asked.

"Indirectly, yes. I don't get around much. But I make an appearance now and then, especially when it's important. And right now, nothing is more important."

Aaron looked into the eyes of the man standing in front of him. They seemed familiar, giving him comfort and fear at the same time. It was almost overwhelming.

"Who are you?" Aaron asked.

"Let's just say a friend of a friend. For now."

Aaron had learned to live with the vagueness of a new visitor, so he went with it. "Alright, *friend of a friend*. How can I help you?"

"Our friend, Carter, is in trouble, and the only ones who can help him are right here, right now. I've looked at this from every angle, and I have no other choice but to come to you for help."

Aaron looked back and forth at who was watching them. "Are you an angel too, friend of a friend?"

"You can say that."

"Where have I heard *that* line before? I'll take it as a yes." Aaron chucked. "And Carter needs my help?"

"He is lost."

"How's that?" Aaron asked. "How can an angel of the Lord be lost?"

"He's not a heavenly being. He is earthbound, so he assumes the same temptations and risks humans face. It's one of the drawbacks that earthbound angels accept when they receive their assignments. It helps them empathize. But it also carries the inherent risk of falling into human emotions. That's what happened with Carter. We need your help to bring him back."

"Why me?"

"One, he connected with you when he oversaw Deborah's case. And two, to be perfectly honest, you're here right now. Proximity has it's benefits," the angelic being shrugged.

"Do you know where he is?"

"I haven't looked in on him lately, but last time I saw him, he was in the park."

"That's where Derrick saw him," Aaron explained.

"Yes, I witnessed that interaction. Derrick was almost injured there. We had other messengers on guard that kept him safe. But he needs an earthbound guide. He needs Carter for the Reminders to be effective."

"What do you need me to do?"

"Find Carter and convince him to complete his assignment," the visitor said, tilting his head.

"What makes you think I have that much influence?"

"Because you're one of his success stories. It's what he needs to see right now."

Aaron sat, weighing the angelic being's words. Jasmine walked by, refilling his tea and exchanging concerned glances between the three of them. Aaron waved her off.

"Is there anything else I can do?"

"Now that you mention it?" the man picked up a backpack from the floor that Aaron had not noticed before. He pulled out a worn shoe box. Aaron immediately recognized it.

"That's Carter's shoebox," Aaron said. "Is that what he holds his Little Reminders in?"

"It is," the visitor said, placing the shoebox on the counter in front of Aaron.

Aaron could only stare at it. That box once held the Bible with a decorative shell that now sat on his nightstand, the two cookie cutters that he and Pop use to make the cross-shaped cookies for Easter, it may have even held those Coke glasses that were on the shelf above their head right now. Aaron looked up at the glasses, then found the nerve to touch the box.

"How is Carter's box going to help me find him?"

"There are still Reminders in it he hasn't placed yet."

"For Derrick?"

"Yes," the angel began, then took a deep breath. "However, I'm wondering if this goes beyond Derrick. I don't look inside the boxes; it's not for me to know. That's between the Lord, the angel in charge, and the soul we are trying to minister to. But I feel in my heart that this one is different. Perhaps this

Little Reminder case could be just as much for Carter as it is for Derrick. But the only way to find out is for someone to open the box and look. I cannot be that person—or being. I shouldn't even know what's in it. Now that I have passed it on to you, it's now your responsibility to complete Carter's work and to finish this Little Reminders assignment."

"How will I know what to do or when to do it?"

"The same way Carter did. God will lead you."

"It's that simple?" Aaron asked with a smirk and raised eyebrows.

"Of course not. One needs to believe that God is directing them. You must have faith in what you're trying to accomplish. And you should act without questioning what God is directing you to do."

"That doesn't seem so difficult," Aaron said, rubbing his chin and again staring at the shoebox.

"There is one more detail. There's a time factor."

Aaron's head spun toward the angel.

"Don't stress out. You have over a month. Roughly until Thanksgiving. I don't know why the dates are set the way they are, I just convey them. And there's no hard-and-fast date. You just have four weeks to deliver the items in the shoebox."

"I understand," Aaron said.

"Now, the trick is to deliver these at the most opportune time, when they would make the biggest impact on the individual. So, you may have to do a bit of investigating and a little bit of spying. I can send you some information, about family and other history."

"Send me?"

"Yes. I can send you an email with information on Derrick. It would be easier than just telling you straight out."

"You can do that? Angels can do that?"

Aaron's visitor laughed. "What do you think we sit up there on clouds with our harps strumming them all day? We're well connected. We need to be with all the prayer requests coming in and answers going out."

Aaron nodded. What he really wanted was to be taking notes; this was good enough stuff for a piece in the *Gazette*.

"We need to get started right away. Everything you need is in the shoebox. I believe the items are numbered as to their order of placement. Carter usually does that to bring significance to each item. I'll be praying for you. I suggest trying to find Carter first. Try and convince him to complete his assignment. If not, then it'll be up to you to help Derrick with his Little Reminders and direct him toward his path back to God."

Aaron shook hands with the angel, and he looked again at the shoebox. "No worries, I have it under control. You can count on me, sir. If you do stumble upon him, any help finding him will be appreciated."

After the angel left, Aaron opened the box. There were fewer items than he expected. The largest was a worn Bible. It nearly resembled Deborah's shell Bible he discovered at the flea market. The memory swallowed him as he remembered Deborah's story behind the shell with Pop. He choked back tears. After considering his latest conversation with Derrick, Aaron was convinced this Bible needed to be the next reminder. And it would need to be soon. But he needed Carter's help on how to deliver it best. But, where was Carter?

Chapter
Ten

Aaron remembered Deborah saying something about libraries in addition to the parks. Derrick had already confirmed that Carter loved libraries. He had been to four of the larger ones in the city that Friday morning, passing along Carter's description to the librarians. Two of them remembered a man matching the description but hadn't seen him in years. The two downtown were the most helpful. At the Central location where their incident occurred, the librarian stated the man had been there within the last week. The second Houston library said Carter had been in the day before. Aaron was getting close. The second location was just a couple of miles from the diner. *Was he on his way there?*

"Are you sure it was him?" Aaron asked. "Dark tweed coat and brimmed cap?"

"Yeah. He's in here quite a bit. Sits over there," the clerk pointed to a booth in the back corner, "and reads. He keeps to himself, so we never need to bother with him. Didn't know his name until you just said it."

"So, he never speaks to anyone?" Aaron asked out of curiosity because the Carter he knew could talk an ear off.

"Not that I'm aware of. I remember him because he asked about the hours changing."

"Interesting," Aaron said, looking back at the booth. "And you said he was in here last week?"

"Yep. A week ago today. He seemed rather upset now that I remember. He didn't read much that day. Just sat in his booth and stared out the window there."

"Did he stay long?"

"No, not at all. We were about to close. He was in here for about an hour until we had to remind him of our hours. He was very polite and left peacefully."

"And he hasn't been here since?" Aaron asked.

"I haven't worked every day, so I can't be sure."

Aaron looked back at the empty corner and nodded. He thanked the library clerk and left.

The circle had been tightening. *Could it be that simple?*

Aaron drove back to the deli out of exhausted frustration and curiosity if Carter would be there. Deborah said he had a fondness for desserts. Maybe the cobbler had brought him home.

It being Friday, it was Supreme Pizza Sandwich Day. It was one of Pop's pride-and-joys. The sandwich was a twist on the sauce he used for the Spaghetti Sub—something only he knew and swore he would take to his grave. Erica had once told him it was Brown Sugar and Red Wine Vinegar, but he wasn't sure if she had witnessed it or was palate rouletting. It was sweeter. He hoped that Pop would someday share it with the world, so his legacy could live on.

The sweet aroma of pizza sauce and fresh cobbler danced

with each other as Aaron entered the deli. He saw Pop's top hat swooping back and forth through the server's window. His eyes popped up, then a face, giving Aaron a fatherly smile. Aaron returned the gesture and scanned the room. The girls were, as usual, busy with the crowd. It was slowing down, being after 1:00, and the office clerks were already gone. The room was half-filled with nursing scrubs and second-half office staff.

Then there he was, his back toward Aaron. The collar of his tweed coat was most recognizable, the brim of the hat, unmistakable. Carter Jennings sat in the back corner booth. How long he had been there? Perhaps all day. *Was he waiting for me?* It sounded like something Carter would do. Aaron approached the counter and called Pop around.

"Aaron, my boy," Pop said, spatula still in his hand. "What can I do for you?"

"Hey, Pop. Sorry to bother you, I know you have a heavy wheel."

"Anything. Whatcha need?"

"The man in the corner booth." Aaron nodded toward him. "In the tweed. Do you know how long he's been there?"

"Hmm, Table 13. I'm not sure. He looks familiar, though. Should I know him?"

"Yeah, we know him," Aaron said. "Don't worry about it. I was just curious when he came in. He's an old friend. Didn't want to have him waiting forever for me."

"Okay. Well, I better get back to my flattop. Customers await, and I have another pot of secret sauce on the estufa. Mmmm, mmmm mmmm, it is good, Aaron, my boy."

Aaron laughed as Pop darted back through the swinging door. He poured himself a glass of tea and inched his way toward Carter, Derrick's Bible in hand. He didn't feel comfortable with the whole shoebox thing, much less approaching Carter with it. He wasn't sure how he would react to him having it. *One step at a time. One Reminder at a time.*

"It's about time. I was about to give up on you," Carter said without turning around.

"I was about to say the same thing on the street until I realized where you were going." Aaron stopped behind Carter, just out of view.

"We all circle back to what's familiar."

"What was wrong with your library?

"All I could see was that boy's face. And that boy's face led me to his mother's."

Aaron stepped into view. Carter looked up at him. He hadn't aged a day. Same over-stubbled beard, same white hair peeking out from under his tweed hat, same piercing grey eyes. The only change was some of the glow that had lit up a room had dimmed.

"May I sit with you?" Aaron asked.

"You're the one I'm waiting for. Please sit," Carter said, nodding to the seat.

Aaron plopped into the booth with an, "Oof," and took a drink of his tea. He placed the Bible on the chair beside him, out of view. He was not ready to play that card just yet. He wanted to get Carter's side of the story before letting him in on the visitor's plan.

"How have you been, Carter. Long time no see."

"I've seen better days," Carter said with little hesitation. He sipped at his coffee and looked over his shoulder to the cook's window. "I see the Davies are doing exceptional."

"Indeed, they are."

"I hear you're a partner now."

"Yes, sir. Pop and I are co-owners. I still work with the paper, though, part-time."

"Sorry about Mrs. Davies. She was a sweet lady."

"Yes, Mom's passing was hard to accept. Especially so close to losing Deborah. But Pop took it in stride. He's just high on life and knows God has a plan in everything, even loss. He seems stronger than ever. But I do keep an eye on him. Losing two loved ones so close together has to do something to you."

Carter nodded. "I'm glad you're here for him. I'm glad God's reminders touched your life. He needed you as much as you needed him."

"And I have you to thank more than anyone. If it weren't for you, I wouldn't be here today. You guided me to where I am right now. Your obedience to God's direction led me to become who I am today."

Carter shook his head. "No, that was you. Deborah Davies was my assignment. You were just along for the ride and happened to find your way as a side effect."

"Regardless. I have you to thank for *my* return to Christ. God used me in Deborah's life, and it turned two hearts back instead of one. It doesn't matter if Deborah was your Little Reminder or not, you impacted and changed my life as well. It shows that God uses you in more ways than you think."

Carter nodded and was quiet. He sipped his coffee, then looked down at the cup. "I don't know what you want from me, Aaron."

"I think it's more about what *you* want from *me*," Aaron clarified.

Carter looked up to him, his white brows furrowed.

"You know what I'm talking about. What brings you here?"

Carter shrugged. "Familiarity, I suppose. It's the last place I felt I belonged."

"Can you elaborate?"

"I'm not sure if I can in terms you could understand," Carter said, looking up to the ceiling.

"What, is it an angelic thing?"

"In a way."

"I think I can try; go ahead."

"In my position, when I'm sent to help individuals, a level of connection is made. Call it *spiritual* if you want. I suppose that would be the closest explanation I could compare it to. It helps God work within each heart. But it allows me to see into people to know just how to react and help them. That connection runs deep, and sometimes it's hard to let go once the assignment is complete."

"Because of your duality; your human side here, versus the angelic side you gave up to remain here."

Carter's eyes squinted. "Precisely. How you know that, I don't know, but that's right on the money. For some individuals, it's harder to break that bond. That tie remains. I have experienced it just a couple of times."

"And the reason you're here is that Deborah was one of them."

"It's why you and I are sitting together now, yes," Carter said, sipping his coffee.

"And Derrick Anders is the other. Or rather Angela Robertson."

Carter nodded.

"And what happened with Angela Robertson?"

Carter shook his head. "She died."

"I know that. Derrick has told me all about it. He told me about the night he saw you three years ago with his mom."

Carter's head shot up. "What have you told him?"

"Nothing," Aaron said, holding up his hands. " He doesn't know who you truly are. All I've told him is that he needs to talk to you and follow your instructions. That's all."

Aaron felt studied through Carter's glare. "You can't tell him the truth, Aaron. It'll ruin everything. He needs to draw closer to God of his own volition. Telling him could drive him further away."

"Then you need to get back to work, Carter," Aaron said, pointing at him. "Sitting here sulking only gives the enemy time to drive him further from God. Remember, this is your task to complete."

Carter's eyes went back to his cup, rotating it in its saucer. He exhaled. "I'm not sure if I can, Aaron."

"Then perhaps you need a little help from a friend." Aaron placed the Bible that was at his side on top of the table. Carter's neck cocked to the side as his eyebrows furrowed, then a burst of recognition lit up his face, "Derrick's Bible? But how…"

"Don't worry about how I got it. Just know that you're not alone now. You and I will work on this together."

"This was in my—"

"Shoebox. Yes, I know."

Carter looked down at the Bible. He picked it up and held it with familiarity. Aaron remembered that Derrick said his mom and Carter had a discussion in his living room. If his mom was an assignment, could there have been more than one? This Bible could have more of a history than anyone knew.

"Let's say we are in this to help Derrick together. You don't have to do this alone. You helped save my life. The least I can do is help you save another."

Carter looked up at Aaron, and for the first time, a smile peaked across his face. It wasn't the glowing beam he was used to, but it was a hint of the Carter that once was. Maybe it was the hope Aaron was giving him. He had made the effort that the visitor had instructed him to, now the results seemed to be taking effect. Aaron just hoped it would be enough to reignite the fire that was once in Carter to complete his assignment and save Derrick's soul.

Chapter

Eleven

"Hey Derrick, it's Aaron. I was wondering, does the school still give you guys extra credit for volunteering for Thanksgiving at kitchens for the holidays?"

"Yes, sir, they do. Why, do you need help?"

"Yes, we do. I'm not sure if you know, but Pop started a Thanksgiving tradition a few years ago to feed the homeless. We started with about thirty. Last year we had over one hundred. This year we expect 150, maybe more. We're preparing now. We usually get quite a few college students to help out on the day of, but I could use some help leading up to it. Would you be up for it?"

"Sure. I need some volunteer hours to graduate. Not that I wouldn't do it anyway. But sure, I would love to help. What do you need me to do?"

"Pop and I are grateful. Actually, I need help starting later today. I'm stuck at the paper all day against a deadline. I was supposed to pick up a few boxes of napkins from HA Restaurant Supply. Do you know where that is?"

"No, but I have a maps app on my phone. I'm sure I can find it."

"Wonderful. I really appreciate your help, Derrick. I know you have a small car. There should be three boxes, but they aren't too big. Should be no problem fitting in a trunk."

Aaron could hear Derrick laughing on the other end of the phone. He assumed it was over the state of his trunk. He knew for two reasons. One, he was a single man once and knew the condition of a bachelor's backseat area. And two, that was where he placed the Bible that Derrick would find as the second Little Reminder at Carter's suggestion.

"What are their hours?" Derrick asked.

"Regular business, I believe. Your map search may give more answers than than my memory."

"Gotcha. I'll check it out before I head into work this afternoon. Can I bring them by on Monday? I don't believe you're open tomorrow."

"Yeah, Monday is fine. And you can try the Spaghetti Sub."

Derrick was laughing again. "It's a date. Talk to you later," he said, hanging up.

"Excellent job, Aaron," Carter said, sitting in the passenger seat next to him. He nodded to the scene in front of them. "Now, you hid the Bible where it didn't look like it was placed there, but not hidden to where he would miss it, correct?"

"Yeah, I hid it somewhat like I found Deborah's shell Bible," Aaron said with a sly vibe in his voice.

Carter laughed. "Right. The shell Bible. That discovery was perfect for you. How could I forget about that? That was a close one. I almost had to intervene there. You were moving far too fast for my taste."

"You were there?"

"Of course I was there," Carter said, his glowing smile returning. "I will sometimes make sure deliveries are received, especially when they're not made directly to the one God is seeking to save. Gabriel makes such a fuss, though. He says I make too much contact; that I should drop it and move on to the next Reminder."

"Gabriel?"

Carter's face revealed he may have overstepped his bounds, "He's a friend. We talk about assignments."

"Mmm-hmm," Aaron said. He may have just put a name to a face. "Maybe *Gabriel* has a point. But perhaps getting involved is what has gotten you too connected to Derrick?"

Carter was silent, chewing on Aaron's words. "Perhaps," he admitted. "But I feel my connection helps people become closer to God. It helped Deborah. It helped with you."

"You didn't reveal yourself to me until the end," Aaron said.

"Yes, but it helped you connect all the dots between Deborah, Pop, and yourself. How much did our talk on the bench help you that night?"

Aaron thought back to the night after the community dinner where Carter had appeared to him. Their talk had opened his eyes to many things about himself, his connection to Mom and Pop, and the future. "You helped change my life that night, Carter."

"You see. *My* way of connection helps people. I know it's not by the book, and I'm not talking about *The* Book. I'm talking about general guidelines for how earthbound angels are to behave. But you have to admit, I am effective at what I do."

"Carter. What happened with Angela?"

Carter's eyes went misty. "I don't know. She was fine one day, then the next she was fed up with God."

"According to Derrick, she was a spiritual woman."

"Yes. I know. I was there. I was even wondering why I was assigned to her at times" Carter said.

"If you don't mind me asking, what were her Reminders?".

"A trinket that had been her mom's, a scripture verse bookmark from the doctor who got her into medicine, and a photo of her husband and Derrick were among them."

"The photo. Was it black and white? Mr. Anders is holding him at home, and he's wearing a dress shirt?"

"Yes, that's the one," Carter nodded.

"Derrick's Reminder is that photo. It was tucked into the book you placed."

"Hmm. It would make sense they would have that same Reminder. It's something both of them have been fighting to forget, or rather, get to know."

"So, what do you think could have set her off?"

"Work and life becoming overwhelming; I don't know."

"Why were you there that night?"

"Which night?"

"The night Derrick saw the two of you arguing. He saw your coat and hat. It's what caused him to recognize you that day in the library."

Carter nodded, his eyes showing revelation. He was putting the pieces together. He had no idea why the kid was chasing him so intently, especially that day in the park when he had almost gotten into an accident.

"She asked me to leave her alone. She said she didn't want any more help. I knew where she lived; I'm an angel of God, I know where every one of my assignments lives. So, I went to her home. I was persuasive enough that she let me in, and yes, things became heated enough for voices to be raised, but we weren't arguing. More like stressful consideration that she needed help. Derrick, or *Rick* as I knew him then, must've overheard us."

"You didn't see her after that night."

"No. And I'm afraid that our disagreement turned her away from God."

"But don't you believe that once you are saved, your soul is guaranteed saved?"

"Yes, but you have to remember, I also have a humanness to my angelic side. I have the ability to doubt. These emotions enable me to empathize. Doubt about the existence of *once saved, always saved* hits me all the time."

"That must be tough to live on both sides of the fence like that," Aaron said. He understood having the assurance but still living in doubt. But being an angel and living with that must've been difficult.

Carter nodded toward the house they were staking out. Derrick had finally made an appearance.

"About time," Aaron said, adjusting in his seat. "Not sure how much more my back can take. I'm not as young as I used to be."

A question rose in his mind, and he turned to the angel. "How old are you anyway, Carter?"

"To be honest, I don't know anymore. I stopped counting a long time ago. I was here before your parents were born. Probably before their parents were born," Carter said, his eyes still locked on Derrick, who was fiddling with his keys.

"So, you don't age? You have looked this way since then?"

"I have aged. But my aging process is different than yours. It's difficult to explain. While I'm here on earth, I age, I should say. One day my assignment will be over, and I'll go back to Heaven."

"Were you sent here as punishment?"

Carter laughed. "No, I volunteered. I wanted to come. There's no sin in Heaven. The punishment came and went with the fall centuries ago. I'm not *earning* my way back into Heaven if that's what you're asking. No, angels who are where I am are all here because we choose to be."

"So, there are more of you?"

"You don't know the half of it," Carter smiled, and his eyes took on a familiar glimmer.

"Wow," Aaron said, then pointed to the scene before them, "Look!"

Derrick unloaded two boxes from the trunk and placed them on the ground. They could see him with his head tucked inside the trunk.

"There was loose clothing toward the back and a laundry basket," Aaron said. I put the Bible toward the back under some of the clothing. When he goes to put the clothing inside the basket, he should find the Bible."

"Nice work, Aaron," Carter said. "You should become a guardian angel."

Aaron laughed. He wasn't quite sure how that worked but sensed that dying had some part in it—he wasn't prepared to cross over just yet. "No, Carter, I'm quite happy where I am. I sense my work here isn't done just yet." He watched Carter out of the corner of his eye to see if his expression changed, just in case. It didn't, to his relief.

"Look," Carter said.

Derrick's body frozen. Something had caught his attention.

"He found it. Yes!" Aaron said with a fist pump.

"Let's see what he does now."

Derrick backed out of the trunk compartment with the Bible in his hand. He was stroking his beard, staring at his find. Then he turned, sat on the trunk's edge, and began to thumb through the pages. After several page flips, he began to read.

"I wonder what passage he's reading?" Derrick said.

"Hopefully, Matthew 11:28," Carter said. I put a bookmark there.

"Come to Me, all you who labor and are heavy laden, and I will give you rest," Aaron quoted from memory.

"It's one he needs to learn. He doesn't fully understand it just yet."

"Just yet?"

"Believers who are struggling always hit a point where they need to choose Christ or choose to go their own way. Derrick isn't at that point yet. These Reminders will build up, and the crux comes later. There will be something that becomes the breaking point."

"Like Deborah's illness."

"Right," Carter said. "She knew going into that surgery there was a chance she wasn't going to come out of it. That was the culmination of everything she had learned; the Bible reading, the support her parents had given her, and the love you had given her. She was at peace. But she had to choose Christ before that point. And she did. Derrick has much to go through before he hits that point. What, I don't know for sure. I have been so blinded by my ability to help everyone the last few years that I've become overconfident and went into this assignment blindly. If I hadn't, I probably would have realized who Derrick was sooner. And I could have backed out of it."

"Why would you want to back out of this?"

"Because I cannot help him the way he needs it."

"And that's why I'm here. That's why I was sent to help you." Aaron realized he had messed up the second he said it.

"You what?" Carter's head spun around, his eyes widened, and began to bore holes in him.

"Carter..."

"Who sent you??"

"I—I don't know," Aaron said, which was the truth, even though he had figured it out who his angelic contact was.

"Gabriel came to you, didn't he? He's not supposed to do that. It's breaking the rules. He knows that."

"Honestly, Carter. I don't know who it was. He never said his name. He just asked me to help you. And I said I would. You mean a lot to me, and I didn't like to see you hurting."

"I'm *not* hurting, Aaron. I'm fine," Carter said. He was now fidgeting in his seat.

"Carter. Let's focus on Derrick. He needs our help."

"You want to help him? He's all yours, because I can't help him. I'll lose him the way I lost his mother," Carter said, opening the car door.

"That wasn't your fault. It was a car accident. You couldn't help that."

"I should have!" Carter screamed.

There was silence in the car for a long while. Aaron didn't know how to respond. It was Carter who spoke next. "Why would God allow that?"

"You know why, Carter. People die. Deborah had to die. So did Angela. It's part of life."

"Not for Angela. Not for Angie."

"Carter," Aaron said, with a tone of soft recognition. All of a sudden, everything made sense. Carter had fallen in love with Angela Robertson.

Chapter
Twelve

Derrick was relieved by Aaron's offer. He had been wondering where he would get his volunteer hours. He'd been dreading having to call around to find them and had waited so long his options were thin. Aaron had been a saving grace. Derrick had to laugh at the thought of the words; interesting his mind chose them. He had spent so much time around Aaron that the church was spilling over into his thought pattern.

It occurred to him that if he had to load up boxes, he needed to put them somewhere. If they were big his backseat may not hold them. It would be best to have his trunk available just in case. He grabbed his keys and headed to his car.

Luckily, the items in his truck were primarily boxes of clothing he had intended to drop into a donation station, but there never seemed to be a convenient time. Derrick pulled the boxes out and set them aside. As he gathered the loose clothing, his hand hit a hard object. He pulled the item out. It was a book. But not any ordinary book—it was a Bible. But not any ordinary Bible—it was his mom's Bible. He stood frozen in disbelief.

How did this get in here?

Derrick forgot all about his cleaning expedition and sat on the edge of his car. He opened the Bible and thumbed through the pages, remembering his mom reading her devotionals. He came to a bookmark. It was in Matthew. There was a verse highlighted.

"Come to Me, all you who labor and are heavy laden, and I will give you rest."

Rest. Derrick felt he certainly could use some of that right about now. He felt spread as thin as tissue paper.

All this time, the Bible he had given up searching for was in his trunk. But it didn't make sense. He had been tossing clothes in it for over two years. He should have seen it before now. He looked back at the trunk and sifted through the small pile that remained, wondering what other treasures that pile might contain. Nothing was there. A shout turned his head. A car was parked across the street, but with the sun's glare, he couldn't make out if anyone was in it. It was time to get back inside and get ready to face his day.

Derrick had to laugh when he picked up the boxes of napkins. They could've fit in his passenger seat and floorboard. But the company also included utensils Aaron had not mentioned, which added additional boxes that fillied the trunk space. The attendant said they had received extra and wanted to provide Mr. Davies with a blessing.

"Pass it on," the bubbly clerk said.

Derrick smiled and responsed, "I will. God bless you."

He wasn't sure why he said that, but he didn't want to not say anything.

He called Aaron to let him know of the good fortune, just in case he was trying to find utensils from another source. Aaron said they had planned to use what they had on hand at the deli. Derrick reminded him he would bring the items by Monday after class and said goodbye.

Breonna's Honda was in the lot when he arrived. Instead of parking under the lamppost as he had always done, he parked next to her. He was nervous about seeing her as they hadn't spoken much after their moment in his car. Due to conflicting schedules, this would be the first shift they had worked together since. He took a deep breath and walked through the front doors. Brian had a knowing grin on his face when he walked past the registers. What he seemed to know was beyond Derrick. He hadn't mentioned their moment to anyone. Had she?

Derrick didn't see Breonna as he walked to the back to clock in, nor on his way to the register. He felt both saddened and relieved at the same time. He had no idea what he was going to say to her. Nor did he have the time to say it. He input his numbers on the register and started to take customers—none of them had a tweed hat or coat. Brian was too busy to chat, but he would throw an occasional smirk his way, looking as if he were about to burst with information. Derrick was not looking forward to their conversation.

The line eventually slowed to a trickle, then to one or two, then no one. Once Brian's line was clear, he crossed his arms waiting for Derrick to complete his final transaction.

"Have a good day, Mr. Johnson. Keep an eye on your email. You'll receive a notification when your book is in."

"Thanks, son," Mr. Johnson said, leaving the two cashiers to their inevitable conversation.

Derrick locked his register and turned to Brian. "Okay. Let's have it. Why all the smirks since I walked through the door?"

"Breonna Greene," Brian said and not another word.

"What about her?"

"Kathleen said you two were here alone after everyone left the other night."

Kathleen. The bookstore gossip. It never occurred to him that she worked that night and left before he and Breonna did, leaving them alone. Derrick shook his head. *How many people has she told? What has poor Breonna gone through the past several days?*

"Brian. You should know better than to listen to Kathleen. Remember the crap she tried to start with you and Jennifer not too long ago?"

Jennifer was a barista at the coffee shop. Brian had spent too much time one week in the coffee shop, and Kathleen started a rumor saying he had a thing for her. It nearly got back to Kelly until Jennifer ended it because she was married. She filed complaints with HR which nearly got Kathleen fired.

Brian should've known better, and honestly, so should Kathleen, even if it was true that he and Breonna were alone together.

Brian's Cheshire grin fell. He knew Kathleen's reputation. "Okay, you're right. But you both worked, and she did say you two were still here when she left."

"Yes, we were the last two here. Her brother was late picking her up. All I did was wait with her until he got here. That's all. Nothing happened," Derrick said. He knew it was a half-truth. Nothing happened. They didn't go out. They didn't make out in his car. But they did agreed to possibly see each other at a later date. That put an unexpected smile on his face.

"Ah-ha!!" Brian saw Derrick's slip.

Dang it. Now, what was he to do? "Nothing happened, okay? We thought her brother abandoned her. I was about to take her home. We made it to my car, and while my car was warming up, he showed up. Nothing happened."

"Did you ask her out?" Brian asked, his grin returning.

Derrick gave up. "Okay, yes, I did. We were going to get something to eat that night. But like I said, her brother showed up."

"And nothing since?"

"No. Nothing since."

"Why not?"

Derrick thought about his last several days. He couldn't admit he had been chasing an old man in tweed around town. He didn't want to sound like a lunatic. "I've been busy with midterms. I've also been busy at a local deli to make up my volunteer credit hours for school."

Brian nodded. The answers seemed to suffice. "Well, just so you know, she's been glowing more than usual. Especcially today. So, whatever *did* or *didn't* happen, you sure made an impression. She keeps on checking the time."

"Really?" Again, Derrick tipped his hand with a grin.

"See, there you go as well," Brian pointed to him. "Whatever you two don't have going on sure is going on well. Keep it up." Brian went back to his register and took the next customer. Derrick logged out and took the return cart to the floor, butterflies swarming in hoards.

Derrick's cart seemed a bit heavier than usual. He looked over the titles, and they all seemed to be nonfiction, which just happened to be within Breonna's section. Derrick looked over his shoulder to see an amused smirk on Brian's face. *That evil, conniving; brilliant mastermind.* Brian looked up at him and winked. Derrick smiled and shook his head, but a smile creased his lips. Well, returns were returns, and his work needed to be done. He wondered what stories laid behind the books in his cart today.

It took thirteen books before he got a response. He had almost resigned to finishing the cart at a normal pace to get the job done and move on to other projects. But after placing the Jack Reacher novel *The Hard Way* onto the shelf, he heard the shuffling of feet and a soft clearing of a throat. He turned to see the smile he missed.

"Hey, Breonna."

"Hi, Derrick. Looks like you have quite a few books today."

Derrick smirked. "Yes. It seems we have a few friends in high places." He nodded to the front desk, out of view, but she got the hint from her nod.

"Yeah, so I've heard." She looked down to her feet.

"I'm sorry for whatever you've had to go through the past few days. I don't know what Kathleen has tried to start."

Breonna's smile left her face. Her eyes never left the ground. "It's alright. People know better than to listen to what Kathleen says since the barista incident."

"I know, but it's still out there. I don't want you to get hurt by it," Derrick said, lowering his head and stooping a bit to try and get her to meet his eyes, which she did. "So, how have you been? Otherwise? Did you rip your brother a new one when you got in the car that night?"

Breonna's smile returned, along with a laugh that made Derrick dizzy. All of the times she had stood next to him, all the stories he had brushed aside, and right before him was one of God's most beautiful creatures. How could he have not noticed any of this sooner?

"No, the fear on his face when I got in the car was enough," Breonna laughed. "He had been talking with the youth pastor after service. I couldn't hold that against him. Remember, I mentioned he's struggling. If it meant him getting closer to God and asking questions, I'd stay stranded for a hundred days. Plus, I had good company." Breonna stroked Derrick's arm with her finger and looked up into his eyes.

Derrick smiled behind his reddening face, "It may not have been a date, but it sure felt like one," he admitted. "It was just as nerve-racking."

Breonna laughed again. "I know, right?"

"But we need to do it right. Everyone here is talking about us. May as well give them something to talk about," Derrick smiled, raising an eyebrow.

"Is that your way of asking me out?"

"I've already asked you out," Derrick reminded. "And you said yes. I have a raincheck, remember?"

Breonna laughed. "Yes, I do remember a raincheck in there. So when and where?"

Derrick thought about it. He wasn't sure about her family and church schedule, and he didn't want to put her in an awkward position by asking.

"I know you have church tomorrow. But what does your schedule look like for lunch on Monday before class? I know a great sandwich shop."

"I have an early class, but I'm out at noon. I have to be here at three. I can meet you at one?"

"Great," Derrick said. "It's a place on the south side of town.

I'll get you the directions. It's where I'm doing my volunteer credit hours. They have amazing sandwiches. I've eaten there a few times already."

"What makes them so special?" Breonna asked.

Derrick didn't want to spoil the surprise or get a *No* because a Spaghetti Sub didn't sound all that appetizing to him either, but if it were anything like the Meatloaf Sandwich, it would be amazing.

"Just trust me, you'll be blown away."

Chapter
Thirteen

Derrick awakened a little after 8:00 and stared at the ceiling. Should he get up and go to church? He had to admit he enjoyed part of the service the previous week, but he still wasn't sure religion was for him. It didn't matter if he went or stayed in bed, it wouldn't change his view of who God was. He believed God was up there, but was busy dealing with the bigger issues of life. The little things like schooling and the legal issues surrounding his house didn't matter to Him. Derrick also didn't believe attendance in a building mattered much either. *It was more of a membership than anything, anyhow*, he thought as he rolled over and went back to sleep.

Derrick pulled up to Davies Deli with a weight of guilt upon his shoulders. He was tired and restless from Sunday afternoon. It was well after 1:00 when he woke up after sleeping in. The heaviness immediately hit him, and he carried it throughout the day. Lunch didn't taste the same, the ballgame on TV didn't bring him the joy he usually felt, and the rest he would typically gain from the weekend didn't come. He gave up early and was in bed just after nine o'clock. Now it was Monday morning, and he was shaking it off and ready to start fresh and new.

It was still early, and parking was light in front of the converted and expanded double wide. Derrick hoped Breonna was tech-savvy enough to find Davies Deli and street smart enough to believe the place she saw was, in fact, the place he asked her to meet him. The deli was not in a prime location. He looked for her Honda, but there was no sign of her. Once inside, he found Aaron at his usual spot.

"Hey, Aaron. Where do you want these napkins and utensils?"

"Just put them by the kitchen door," Aaron replied, pointing at the swinging door and the counter where the waitresses' drinks had been the first day he had visited.

"Peter," Aaron called to a young man exiting the kitchen with a bus tub. "Can you help my friend here? He has a few boxes for the banquet."

Peter acknowledged and followed Derrick to his car. They brought in the boxes, and Peter went back to bussing tables while Derrick joined Aaron at the counter. Jasmine brought him a tea with a lemon and three sugars. Derrick nodded in approval.

"Impressive," Derrick said. "They pay attention. I've only been here once, and they remember how I take my tea."

"That's Pop. He only hires the best. He makes sure the girls know their stuff. He knows how to weed out the bad from the good. Calls it a sixth sense. You should have seen Erica when she worked here. She would see a regular walking in from the parking lot and have their order on the wheel before they were even seated."

"Speaking of regulars. I have a date coming in this after-noon. Impress her enough and she may become a regular. You've already won me over. If this Spaghetti Sub is what it's cracked up to be, you may have another loyal customer."

"Did-eye hear someone say Spaghetti Sub?" Pop swung through the double doors.

"Yes, Pop," Aaron said through a hearty laugh, "Derrick came in today especially for your Houston-famous Spaghetti Sub. He even attracted a date for it."

"Fabulous. My DeeDee absolutely loved the Spaghetti Sub. She inspired the sauce. However, I can't tell you how. It's a family secret," Pop said, placing his finger in front of his lips. He followed with a smile. "It was a pleasure meeting you, Mr. Derrick." Pop shook his hand then darted back into the kitchen. "Just let me know when you're ready, and I'll whip it up," Pop said, his eyes popping through the window.

Derrick couldn't help but laugh. Aaron followed. "That's Pop," Aaron said, flourishing his hand in front of him. "So, is this another student at the college?" Aaron asked, then snapped his fingers. "Oh, wait, is this the coworker you were talking about?"

"Yes, Breonna," Derrick said. "That's one thing that makes me nervous about dating her. I've never been one for mixing romance with employment."

"I get it. What if things go sour?"

"Exactly. Then you have to see each other every day. No bueno," Derrick said, shaking his head.

"Okay, I love these stories. It's the writer in me. C'mon, let's go sit down, and you can tell me how it happened."

Derrick looked to the door, then out the windows. With no sign of Breonna, he followed Aaron to their stools. "Alright.

I've told you about our mutual interest. I've been pushing it aside for a while now. But one evening, something just clicked inside, and I noticed her. It began with her smile." Derrick's eyes must have lit up, because Aaron began to laugh.

"Yeah. You definitely like this girl. You have it written all over your face."

"Can I finish?" Derrick said.

"Sorry, sorry. Go ahead," Aaron said through a laugh.

"Well, her brother had her car the other night and pretty much left her stranded at work. So, I offered to take her home. We get to my car, and while waiting for it to warm up, we get to talking. I get the nerve to ask her if she wanted to grab something to eat. She says yes. But then her brother finally showed up, and she ended up going home. With our conflicting schedules, we barely saw each other until Saturday night. And I asked her out for lunch today."

"And not yesterday?"

"She goes to church. I didn't want to bother her on a church day."

"You could have gone with her."

Derrick was silent. He didn't know how to respond to that. To his benefit, Aaron responded for him

"No, I suppose it's a bit early to be taking that big of a step. You have your church, and she has hers. Too many questions this early in the game could complicate things."

Derrick nodded. He hoped Aaron wouldn't ask about his day yesterday. He didn't want to reveal that he didn't go to church. He was embarrassed enough as it was, although he didn't know why he felt so guilty. It was just church.

As luck would have it the door chime rang, and a beautiful customer walked through the door with a confused and amazed look on her face—the look of a first-time visitor to Davies Deli.

Derrick excused himself and met Breonna at the door.

"Hey, Breonna. Any problems finding the place?"

"Not at all. I was a bit confused if I was in the right place," Breonna said, looking out the window. "It's very—unassuming."

"That it is. I said the same thing on my first visit. But as you can see once you step in, it's far more interesting indoors. And just wait until you taste the food."

Breonna noticed the billboard sign at the register. "Spaghetti Sub? You've got to be kidding me."

"Told you it would be interesting. If I told you that we'd be going out for a Spaghetti Sub on Saturday, what would you have said?"

"I would have called you insane and second-guessed your taste."

"Exactly. But now you can second guess it all you want; I have you here. You don't have to eat it if you don't want to. Pop has many other sandwiches to choose from."

"Pop?"

"The owner of the deli," Derrick pointed back to the window where Pop's hat showed he was hard at work.

"The co-owner, Aaron, is over here. C'mon, I want you to meet him." Derrick took Breonna's hand and walked her over, not realizing he was taking her hand for the first time.

Aaron had a smirk on his face when they arrived; his eyes fixed on their hands, he quickly refocused onto Derrick's face. It was then that Derrick realized where his hand was. He turned to Breonna, and her smile was as wide as the Rio Grande. He didn't know if he should let go and apologize or go with it. He chose the latter.

"Aaron. This is Breonna Greene. Breonna, this is Aaron Stephenson. He is co-owner of the diner."

Breonna and Derrick let go of their palm embrace, and she shook Aaron's hand.

"Pleasure to meet you, Breonna. I've heard much about you," Aaron said with a sly smile to Derrick, turning both Derrick and Breonna several shades of pink.

"I'm not sure what to say to that," Breonna said, "but nice to meet you, too, and what on earth is a spaghetti sub?"

"Pop has an inventive mind," Aaron explained. "He loves to play with different flavors of food, so he creates different types of meals, only in sandwich form. Thus, you get a Baked Chicken Sub, a Meatloaf Sandwich, and the Spaghetti Sub."

"Meatloaf Sandwich?" Breonna said, eyebrows raised.

"Saturday's special," Derrick and Aaron said in unison, making Breonna jump.

"Sorry," Derrick said, touching her arm.

"It must be good," Breonna said.

"Life changing," Derrick said.

"Hey!" Aaron said. "That's my line."

They both laughed. Derrick looked to Aaron with raised eyebrows, and he knew what he was insinuating.

"I'll see what I can do. If Pop can do it once, I'm sure he can do it again for his favorite customer."

"Thanks, Aaron," Derrick said. Then he turned to Breonna, "That is, of course, if you were considering it."

"I haven't even sat down and looked at a menu."

"Oh, yeah, right," Derrick said. "We'll find a booth. Thanks, Aaron."

"Not a problem. Just trying to help," Aaron said, laughing.

Derrick led Breonna to a booth. Jasmine arrived and took

Breonna's drink order. The menus were in a wire holder along with the napkin holder. It was a single-paged laminated sheet. Derrick didn't need to look. If she ordered from the menu, he would order the Spaghetti Sub. But if she went for the Meatloaf Sandwich, he would have what she was having.

"Wow. Fried Chicken Sandwich on Thursdays? They sure do have every base covered."

"Yes, and the chicken is fresh and fried here. I haven't had it yet, but I haven't been here on Thursday either. Between school and work, I never get the chance."

"Well, if they can make you a Meatloaf Sandwich today, I'm sure you can get a Chicken Sandwich anytime you want."

Derrick laughed. "Perhaps. But a fried dish could be a bit more complicated."

"I'll be nice and wait. I can be patient. We can always come back on a Thursday," Breonna grinned. "I'll have the Chicken Salad."

"You sure? It's a great sandwich," Derrick said without grasping the full gravity of Breonna's statement.

"I'm sure," she said, her grey eyes meeting his. "So, are you really going to try a Spaghetti Sub?"

Derrick looked back to the kitchen window with concerned eyes. "Aaron says it isn't what you think, so I have to go with him on this one. I turned up my nose at first on the Meatloaf and nearly ended up on the floor, it was so good. I gotta try this one."

Breonna laughed, and Derrick nearly ended up on the floor anyway. He wondered how God could create something so beautiful and get away with it.

"You guys ready?" Jasmine returned with a pad and pen and took their order. For the next fifteen minutes, Breonna and Derrick talked back and forth about work and school. He spoke of his dream of helping kids through the situation he came from growing up in a single-parent home. Breonna told him about getting through the MCATS. She spoke of her overprotective parents questioning every movement outside the home and a younger brother that was on the road to trouble but was at least beginning to ask questions.

Derrick didn't talk about the man in the hat, finding the photo of his father, the book he found in the bookstore, or discovering his mom's Bible. He wasn't ready to get emotional in front of her. He could tell she was getting a bit spiritual with her words, and his eyes began shifting toward the kitchen, hoping for a reprieve. Another subject he wasn't prepared to discuss was religion.

"Yeah, my brother is young, so he thinks the world revolves around his friends and that God comes second. But I think it's just fear. He wants God first but is just scared to say anything out of fear of what his friends would say," Breonna said. She twirled her straw around her near-empty glass of tea. She looked up at him and sighed. "You've been there, Derrick? What would you tell him?"

Derrick sat in stunned silence. He didn't know how to respond. Sure, he was once in Ellis' shoes battling peer pressure, but it was never about Christ. His battle was about his grades or drugs. Two things he was adamant about—good grades, yes; drugs, no. He was so focused he didn't have time for God. He had to get home and take care of house duties, because his mom had jobs or schooling. His life was busyness.

He must've been silent too long, because Breonna began to tear up. Derrick tried to reach for words but came up empty. As joyful and uplifting as her laughter was, her tears were heart-wrenching.

Derrick took a deep breath. He found the counselor inside of him and used his skills to answer. "I would tell him not to give up. You told me he's asking questions. That's a good thing. The best you can do is make sure he asks the *right* people these questions, because right or wrong he'll look for answers somewhere. If it's not from you or your youth minister, it'll be from those friends you're desperate to keep him from. Use his curiosity to your advantage. Talk to him. Don't be afraid of him. Most of all, don't shut him out. If you begin to address his curiosity, he'll continue to go to you instead of his friends. That's the best you can do, Breonna."

Breonna smiled again. "You know, I love it when you say my name."

Derrick laughed. "That whole heartfelt speech and all you got from it is when I said your name?"

"Of course not. I appreciate your words. And you're right. The best thing I can do is be there for him. If I push, it'll only make things harder. I just need to let him know I'm here."

"Exactly."

"You saying my name put the bow on the package."

Derrick smiled. This time, he felt *he* was the one glowing. Jasmine must have noticed, because there was a ring in her voice as she delivered their sandwiches. Breonna was enamored with the creaminess of the chicken salad. Derrick couldn't believe he was now two for two in being blown away by Pop Davies and his imagination with sandwich creation.

Spaghetti Sub?

Genius!

Chapter
Fourteen

It was a new week of classes, midterms were over, and Derreck had passed all his classes with flying colors—even his Parent-Child Relationship course with Mr. Atkins. His paper received high marks. The professor continued addressing him with a double first name, however. It was unnerving at first, but it set him apart from the other students. And after what the librarian said about him, Derrick felt it could be a good thing. He accepted the moniker and wore it as a badge.

"Derrick, Derrick Anders…"

"Yes, Professor Atkins?"

It was like having an uncle who liked to play *pull my finger*. He just had to get used to doing it. Only in the case, the smell was how the other students reacted to the attention.

Ignore them and keep moving forward, Derrick thought.

His paper, "The Effects Society Has on Children in Single Parent Homes," earned him kudos not only from Mr. Atkins but a literary journal his professor had submitted the paper to without Derrick's knowledge. It was a small publication, but Derrick was humbled by the experience and honored that the professor would hold him in such high regard. Derrick tucked the journal into his backpack like he was hiding a secret treasure map that no one but himself should have access to.

He couldn't wait to show it to Breonna—*his work in print!* Not that she would recognize the publication, but his name in print would be exciting enough.

The end of the period came, and the students filed out. Derrick remained in his seat while Professor Atkins stood writing on the board. As if there were eyes on the back of his head, he spoke. "Is there something I can do for you, Mr. Anders," he said, there only being the two of them.

"I wanted to thank you for submitting my paper to the *Family Psychology Journal*," Derrick said, walking to the front of the classroom.

"I like to give credit when it is due, Mr. Anders," Professor Atkins said, taking his eyes off the board. "Your performance on your assignment was exceptional. You earned the grade and placement in the journal."

"What made you choose me?" Derrick asked, hoping for more information along the lines of what Miss Betsy had alluded to in the library.

"Your work spoke to me, Mr. Anders. There aren't many students who can do that. The content was clear, concise, and it showed you had studied the material well."

Derrick let out a small chuckle.

"Did I say something funny, son?"

"With all due respect, sir, most of what I wrote was not studied but lived."

The professor lowered his glasses and looked Derrick up and down, then into his eyes. "Is that right?"

"Yes, sir," Derrick met his stare, "It hasn't been an easy road to get where I am today. Hell, it isn't an easy road I'm on now. But I'm here, and I'm driving it. I'd have it no other way. Sir."

Professor Atkins stared at Derrick for a long moment, then grinned. "That's exceptional, son. I should have known by the depth of your wring that it was more than study. Forgive my short-sightedness. You've earned your placement all the more. It's not easy to talk about where we've come from and how we've overcome such obstacles to succeed in life. Bravo, Derrick. Bravo."

"Thank you, sir. I appreciate it. And I'm honored."

"The honor was mine. I only ask you to continue your studies and remember this moment should the going get tough—uh, *tougher*. I hear there are some hard-asses among the faculty," the professor pursed his lips and looked around in a circle.

Derrick laughed. "You have my word, Professor." Derrick shook hands with the not so hard-assed professor and dodged a couple of second-year students as he left the room.

Derrick felt on top of the world. His grades were better than he had imagined; he was even getting accolades from one of the most demanding professors in the college. He met a woman who had finally given him hope about relationships. Even his employer had seen his challenges and made adjustments to accommodate his difficulties. Yes, life was looking up for Derrick Anders.

But as if the words were spoken too soon, Derrick looked into his rearview mirror and saw the two colors that every driver fears: red and blue. "Damn," Derrick swore. He looked down at his speedometer—no issues there, he was well below the limit. With this traffic, he couldn't speed even if he wanted to.

There was nowhere to pull over. Derrick exhaled roughly. He was near the park where he had seen Carter and remembered the ballfield ahead. He could pull into the lot there. He turned on the flashers to let the officer know he had seen him and coasted into the lot. It was emptier than before, so he quickly parked, turned off his engine, and sat and waited. The officer pulled in behind him.

The officer took his time approaching his window, making Derrick nervous. He looked at his window tags—they were up to date. He thought about his insurance—it was on auto-pay. He was so lost in thought that he missed the officer's walk up to his car until he heard the *tink-tink-tink* of a baton against his window. He jumped and looked to see the officer making the *roll down your window* motion.

"Sorry, officer," Derrick said.

"May I see your license, please," the officer asked in a firm but polite tone.

Derrick reached for his license and handed it to the officer.

"I'll be right back," the officer said, tapping the ID on the car and leaving.

Derrick watched the officer get into his patrol car through the rearview mirror. He sat in his vehicle for what seemed like an eternity. Derrick started to tap on his steering wheel with his thumbs in impatience. *What was taking so long?* He knew his license was valid. He turned twenty-one not too long ago and just received his horizontal license.

After another eternity, Derrick saw the patrolman's car door open and shut through his side mirror. The officer approached his door. "Sir, can you please step out of the vehicle?"

"Can I ask what the problem is, officer?"

"Can you just please step out of your car, sir," the officer said a bit firmer.

Derrick understood and took his next steps carefully—very carefully. His heart was in his throat, and he felt the urge to vomit. He took one look at the officer in his side-view mirror before he opened the door, but he didn't have his hand on his sidearm; that was a good sign. Derrick slowly opened the door.

"Okay, officer, I am opening my door." Derrick opened the door. "I'm stepping out of my car," Derrick stepped out of his car, making sure he kept both of his hands in the officer's line of sight at all times. Still, the officer did not have his hands anywhere near his belt; they were folded across his chest. He had a confused look on his face.

"Son, are you under the impression you are in trouble or something?"

Derrick didn't know what to say. "I don't know. Am I, Officer?"

"I need to show you something back here," the officer nodded his head toward the back of Derrick's car.

Derrick loosened the tension in his shoulders, took a step toward the officer, and followed him to the back of his car. Both men stopped, and although both blinkers were flashing, the red glow on the driver side of Derrick's car was lit, the passenger side was dark. The officer pointed at it.

"You have a taillight out," the officer said.

"Oh," Derrick said. He was a bit embarrassed and a little unnerved.

Why didn't the officer just say so? Why the song and dance? He could just have easily walked up to the window and say, 'Hey, son, I just wanted you to know that you have a taillight out. Get it fixed, have a good day.' But no, he had to drag it out and make it a big deal.

However, Derrick understood that he shouldn't make this a bigger deal than it was. "Yes, officer. I apologize. I was cleaning out my trunk to help out a soup kitchen. I must've knocked it loose," Derrick said, hoping the public service announcement would score some points.

"Pop the trunk," the officer nodded to the car.

Derrick shrugging his shoulders. He figured the officer was attempting to call his bluff. That was okay, he was telling the truth. All the officer would see was an empty trunk. He didn't have time to put back the originally removed boxes. Chances are that's what had happened anyhow. And if it was a burned-out bulb, his story still could attribute to the bad bulb.

"I need to get the key," Derrick said. "Do you want to follow me?"

The officer smirked, "I think I'm okay here. If you try and take off, where are you going to go? Through the park?"

"Riiiight," Derrick looked around as he walked back to the car. The officer did a decent job of boxing him in. He hadn't realized it.

Derrick brought back the keys and tried to hand them to the officer. "Your car, Mr. Anders. I'm good."

Derrick nodded and popped open the empty trunk to the somewhat surprise of the officer. Both men looked over to the electrical wiring of the light. Sure enough, the harness of the fixture had come unplugged. The officer himself reattached it, and the light lit up, good as new.

"What do ya know?" the officer said.

"Yeah, sorry about that. Didn't realize it had come loose."

The officer looked at Derrick with a quizzical look on his face, "Soup kitchen, huh?"

"Well, it's not really a soup kitchen," Derrick said. "It's a deli. Davies Deli. Have you heard of it?"

The officer's face lit up. "Who hasn't? Best sandwiches in town."

"I was taking some stuff over to Pop Davies for his Thanksgiving banquet, and I guess I knocked that wire loose," Derrick said, pointing at his trunk.

"Well, it's fixed now," the officer said with a complete change of tone from when he was *tink-tink-tinking* on Derrick's window.

"Yes. May I leave, Officer? I'm going to be late for work," Derrick asked as politely as he could.

The officer concluded their encounter with a handshake and a written warning that he assured wouldn't go on his record to give to his boss so he wouldn't count him as tardy for the day. Derrick was sure he was trying to make up for his attitude at the beginning of their encounter. Perhaps. Derrick was used to it, but it still didn't mean he was *used to it* when he experienced it. *Apologies don't mean much*, he thought. *They shouldn't need to be given in the first place.*

Derrick arrived at work with time to spare. He didn't need the officer's get out of jail free card. He tossed it in the outdoor bin when he arrived. He went inside, hoping the aroma of coffee and pastries would place him into work mode. They did little to help. Derrick would never mention the roadside assistance to anyone, not even Aaron, who had a big fan in said officer.

Derrick didn't realize how foul of a mood he was in until a certain headband-wearing smile walked around the corner of the aisle he was reshelving. For the first time in a long time, it didn't make him weak in the knees. He pulled a book off his cart and heard a comment, but he paid little attention. It wasn't until he felt a warm hand on his arm that he turned his head.

"Derrick?" Breonna said. She looked at him, eyebrows raised. "Are you alright?"

"I'm fine," Derrick's comment was as dry as sawdust.

"Well, how am I supposed to believe that?" she said, her attempt at breaking down his defenses.

Derrick wasn't sure if he wanted to pour out his soul and explain everything or snap and tell her to mind her own business. "I don't want to talk about it, Breonna," his comment came out firmer than he intended.

"What's wrong with you?" she said, taking a step back.

"I'm sorry," Derrick said, realizing his mistake. "I just don't want to talk about it."

"Well, fine then," Breonna said, her eyes filling with tears as she turned and walked away.

"Breonna," Derrick called as she turned out of the aisle. He watched to see if she would return. When she didn't, he released a heavy huff.

Derrick finished his book stocking and headed back to the register, where a confused Brian was getting rid of a line that had formed. Derrick logged in and helped him through the rush. After the final customer was handed their bag, Brian turned to Derrick shaking his head. "What did you do?"

Derrick remembered how quickly news spread around the workplace. It was like there was a camera in every corner where workers watched what was happening in his life. He tried to play it off, "What are you talking about?"

"Derrick. You always seem to forget that Penny and Breonna are practically best friends. They tell each other everything."

"Even after ten minutes?"

Brian lowered his head. "These are ex-teens we're talking about. They're still learning about life in their twenties. So yeah, texting every detail about life as it happens is still a thing."

Derrick wanted to scream. What started as a pretty good day was not ending so well and was rapidly spinning out of control.

"Okay, so I may have let myself get a little bit upset in front of Breonna."

"A little? Penny said you had Breonna in tears, that you roared at her like a lion."

Roared? Like a lion?

Oh, this wasn't good. He didn't mean for it to turn out like this. The last thing he wanted was for her to fear him.

"I didn't *roar* at her," Derrick thought for a moment. *Yes, I did.* "Okay, yeah, I did get upset, but it wasn't directed at *her.*"

"Well, she seems to think it *was,*" Brian said.

Derrick acknowledged that he would talk with her. Embarrassed, he didn't know what to say. *Roared like a lion?* He couldn't have that on his conscience. It would erase every good memory she has of him. Her tears had already replaced her glowing smile for him, and that was *not* acceptable.

"Where is she?" Derrick asked.

"Coffee shop, I think. She took a break," Brian said, thumbing to their right. "I got you covered. Go."

Derrick made his way around the counter, through the lobby, and into the coffee shop. Breonna was sitting at the front corner, near the window. It was already dark outside, and he could see her reflection in the glass, which meant she could see him as he approached her. He walked up to her, step by step—he didn't want to startle her.

"It would be more dramatic if you had a coffee in your hands for me," Breonna said.

"Would it now?"

"A gentleman always smooths over things with a warm beverage."

"Does he now? You'll have to forgive me. I'm not up on the latest coffee craze. I don't know how you take your coffee."

"No coffee. Too late for coffee. But tea would be nice. Chamomile with lemon, please."

"I'll have your order in a moment, my lady," Derrick said. "Will a suitor be joining you?"

"He may join in a moment—if his manners become more appropriate," she said.

"I'm sure he has taken his head out of his arse and learned his lesson, my lady," Derrick said.

"Then he may join," Breonna said, with a soft sniffle.

Derrick approached her, placed his hand on her shoulder, and kissed the top of her head. "I'm sorry."

Breonna nodded with a sniff, then looked back up at him and smiled. "My tea?"

"Oh, yeah, sure. Coming right up—my lady."

Chapter
Fifteen

I haven't seen him since that night," Aaron said. "And you can drop the cloak and dagger bit. I know who you are, Gabriel. Carter dropped a dime on you."

"I assumed as much," Gabriel said, looking both ways from under his ball cap.

"You look silly, by the way. Even by tourist standards. If you guys are watching us so much, you would think you could blend in much better when you step into the reality of earthly life."

Gabriel shrugged. "This isn't my game. Carter is the guardian. I'm God's Messenger. I don't get to see what happens here too much with all the traveling. And when I'm not here, I am in the presence of the Lord."

Aaron's face lit up. "What's it like? Really?"

"Aaron, there are no earthly words I can use to describe Him. We have angelic words, but I dare not utter them. Not that you would understand them if I did. I wish I could, because it's so exciting. When I'm here, I long to be there. When I am there, I long to share what I have there with those not there. It's why He chose me to be His Chief Messenger."

"Man, I can't wait," Aaron said, slapping the table a bit too loud. It rattled the cup and silverware on the counter, startling the older gentleman further down the counter. Aaron waived in apology, "Sorry, Isaac."

Gabriel laughed at the irony of the man's name. "We need to find Carter. It has been tough to locate him even for me. And that's saying something."

"Yeah. I've checked the libraries and parks, and he hasn't shown up back here." Aaron was nervous about asking the inevitable question. "Has this happened before?"

"What, an earthbound guardian falling in love with the one he's supposed to guide?" Gabriel asked, then pout-shrugged. "Once or twice." From his tone, it sounded like that number could have been a bit more.

"And are there consequences for the angel when this happens?" Aaron was afraid of the answer. He liked Carter. If it weren't for him, he would never have met Deborah. But it occurred to him that if there had been consequences, he would never have seen Carter again in the first place.

"Not generally. It would depend on how far the angel took those feelings. In Carter's case, Angela passed away before anything happened. He lost sight of his goal and thought he could prevent her from passing. He knew it was going to happen. He just didn't know *how* it was going to happen. Her death was as sudden to him as it was to her and Derrick."

"And him not being able to prevent it is what he's so upset about. So, what can I do to help out? Besides trying to find him?"

"Honestly, I don't want you to try and find him. It's too

late for that. What I do need is for you to complete his assignment. You still have the shoebox, right?"

"Yes. He left it in my car that night. I thought he had taken it, but when I got home, the box was still in my backseat."

"Where did you drop him off?"

"Where else? The library. I tried to get him to come home with me, but you know Carter."

"The library or the park; Carter is good there. Leave him be. Don't worry, Aaron. He's not as uncomfortable as you think."

"But with him not at either place, I worry," Aaron admitted.

"It just means he's not at the parks where we're used to seeing him, or he's indoors somewhere," Gabriel suggested.

"True. He could have found a shelter. Which would be a good place to hide out."

"Where Carter is is beside the point right now, unfortunately. We need to complete his mission, and that's Derrick," Gabriel reminded him.

"So, I need to talk to him. What do I say?"

"The Lord will lead you. You just need to keep doing what you've been doing. You've laid a solid foundation so far without even knowing it."

Aaron thought about his conversations with Derrick up till now. If anything, Derrick was still clueless about Carter's true identity. That was a positive. But would he have to reveal their secret since Carter was not around to gently reveal it, or allow Derrick to figure it out as he and Deborah were allowed to through his interaction with them? Maybe he could create a Little Reminder to help him figure it out. Or expound on the ones he already had.

He retrieved the shoebox. There were two Reminders left. One was a cross pendant; the other looked like a skeleton key.

He picked them up and held them. He set the key down. It was time to talk to Derrick about the cross.

Aaron held the cross in his palm as he walked toward the coffee shop. He said a quick prayer for guidance and the words he would say. He knew this needed to be quick. Derrick wouldn't have much time, and this being his workplace, it was his territory; he'd have control. The thought made him laugh. "No, Aaron, God has control," Aaron whispered.

A bell rang as Aaron entered the door. Eyes turned, and an espresso machine grinded. Aaron felt a bit out of place, and while he was barely thirty, he felt much older at that moment. He grinned and nodded at the two twenty-some-things behind computer screens who had looked up at him then back down to their blogs or coursework. The table to his right was empty, so he took a seat and picked up a menu. After finding a coffee that wouldn't have too much sugar, he went to the counter and ordered.

He returned to the table, sat, and texted Derrick that he was in the coffee shop and would wait for him there. His phone buzzed, and a text message appeared.

I'm on my way

Aaron exhaled and looked out the window. It was getting late, and the traffic was picking up. People were out and about, starting their holiday shopping. Banners were already in the windows around town. Even the parking lot had tinseled up lampposts, and Thanksgiving wasn't for another two weeks.

Two weeks. Gabriel's words echoed in Aaron's head.

"Here's your coffee, Aaron," a barista named Raelyn snapped

him out of his daze. She handed him his cup. "You sure you wouldn't care for coffee cake or a cookie this afternoon?"

"No, thank you, Raelyn. I'm fine."

"Just let me know if you change your mind," she said with a smile.

Aaron looked up to see Derrick entering the shop. Standing, he waved him over and shook his hand. "How are you, Derrick? How's the shift?"

"Busy. You would think print books would be forgotten with all the eReaders out there. Nope, they're just as popular as ever," Derrick said, plopping into a chair.

"Thanks for meeting me. I know you've been busy with work and school."

"Not a problem. What can I do for you? Another delivery?" Derrick chuckled.

"Well, now that you mention it, we'll need a few more hands for Thanksgiving, but that won't be for another week or so."

"Sure, that shouldn't be a problem. I'd be glad to help. I may even be able to scrounge up a couple of other hands if you need them," Derrick said, thinking of the campus groups at the college.

"That would be great," Aaron said, then cleared his throat. *Why am I beating around the bush? Just get to it already.* "There's another reason I stopped by," Aaron said, then sipped from his cup.

Aaron was unsure how to begin, but he figured just getting to it would be best. He took a deep breath, released it, and began to speak. "We've been meeting now for a couple of weeks, and we've danced around discussing God. We've talked directly about what He may have in store for your life. We've even touched on what Carter's involvement may be in that. But I may have a bigger role to play in this than I originally assumed. And I now feel that I need to talk to you more about it."

Derrick leaned forward onto the table and folded his hands. "I'm listening."

"There are a few things about me that you don't know. Some things I've been reluctant to share with you because they're personal, but after getting to know you and where you stand personally, I feel I need to share with you." Aaron's hand went to his pocket, holding the cross there. "I knew someone who was once like you. She was a believer *about* God, but she wasn't a believer *in* God. It took a series of events in her life to get her to see the reality of who God was. God sent someone to give her Little Reminders of who He was to cause her to remember who God is. She had a Christian upbringing, too, but lost it along the way."

"And this person knows God now?"

"*Very* intimately. She is with Him today."

Derrick looked puzzled, then his eyes flashed with realization. "I'm sorry. You're talking about Deborah?"

"Yes, she was almost my wife," Aaron said. "You hear Pop talking about DeeDee?"

"Yes."

"That was his daughter, Deborah. We were involved before she passed away."

"How long were you two together before she died?"

Aaron laughed, then went silent. "A month or two. She went fast."

"I'm sorry, Aaron. I didn't know."

"There's nothing to be sorry about. God gave us our time

together. The point of my story is that she had turned her back on God, nearly an atheist. But God sent Little Reminders into her life that directed her back to Him."

"You keep saying *Little Reminders*, as if that should mean something to me. Is there a point to that?"

"Yes, there is. God is always giving us opportunities to turn back to Him. He drops hints to us that remind us of who He is. For Deborah, it was a set of cross-shaped Cookie cutters that reminded her of her grandmother." Aaron took a breath. He was nervous but decided to mention it anyway. "Another was a Bible. I was the one to find it. I feel God led me to find it for her. We were at a rummage sale, well, a flea market, and a vendor was selling it. It had a shell on the cover. It so happened that shells were important to her and Pop."

Derrick's eyes widened. Aaron caught it; he figured it was over the Bible they had placed.

"It is funny you mention rummage sale. Breonna said she found my mom's headband at a rummage sale. Interesting coincidence."

Aaron lowered his head and looked into Derrick's eyes. "Derrick, there are no such thing as *co*-incidences; only *God*-incidences."

"So, you're saying that God put my mom's headband at that rummage sale for Breonna to find?"

Aaron thought about it for a moment, and remembered Mom's Coke bottles and his Bible discovery, and stood on faith. "Yes, Derrick, that's exactly what I'm saying."

Derrick shook his head. "I don't know if I can believe that, Aaron."

Aaron wasn't sure if he should continue. He felt he was losing Derrick. And if he couldn't believe him about a headband, how would he react about the Bible and then about Carter.

"There are many things I went through three years ago that I can't explain. The Bible was one of them. Deborah's cookie cutters, another. But I'm sure you already know what I'm talking about, don't you?"

Derrick squirmed in his chair. Aaron already knew the answer. He just needed Derrick to admit it to move on. But his denial would put the kibosh on the entire meeting. He said a silent prayer for Derrick to submit to the leading and open up to him.

Derrick's mouth opened up, but no words came out. He looked around and lifted a finger. "So, what if I have had an experience or two?"

"Then it would mean God is directing you. It means you have been visited by the same visitor that Deborah and I had. It means that God is sending you the same Little Reminders to bring you back to Him."

"The same visitor?" Derrick said.

"I think you know who I'm talking about, Derrick," Aaron said, raising his eyebrows.

Derrick's face contorted with the sudden realization. "Nawww. Couldn't be. Nawww." Derrick stood and paced the floor. He waved his hands at the floor like he was pushing away a foul smell. "No way," he uttered again in disbelief. He walked toward the door, but stopped, circled back, and sat down. He leaned into Aaron, and almost in a whisper said, "Carter, really?"

Aaron nodded. "Yes. Carter Jennings. He is an angel, and he's been sent by God to guide you back to Him."

Chapter
Sixteen

Derrick was overwhelmed with the information Aaron had dropped on him. *Carter—an Angel?* It didn't make sense.

How could a man who almost looked homeless be an angel? Aaron said God has a purpose for everything, and that even he didn't understand. He said Carter had helped him and Deborah through their relationship and that he had more to talk about.

But Derrick had to complete his shift. He was tempted to walk back to Mr. Lauder and fake sick so he could leave. But Aaron said they had time, and he'd be there after he got off work. He suggested meeting at the deli later.

"It'll be closed, but I'll be there with coffee and fresh cobbler waiting." He didn't have the heart to tell him he didn't drink coffee.

The next couple of hours crawled by, and even Brian noticed his anxiety. "Meeting Breonna after work?" he asked.

"No, a friend," Derrick replied.

"Ahh, the guy you were talking to in the coffee house earlier," Brian said, nodding in its direction.

"Yeah," Derrick affirmed.

"Must be intense. You look like you're about to jump out of your skin."

"I'm fine. He just has news I'm anxious to hear."

"Care to share?" Briand sidled up next to him.

"Not right now, no," Derrick said. How would he even begin to explain.

"Alright. I see how it is," Brian said with an elbow to his side. "I share my future plans."

"Let's just say that a higher power is guarding me."

"Hey, if you want to make jokes about it, then fine. I won't ask anymore," Brian said and went back to his register to help a customer.

Derrick laughed. "If only I were joking," he said and left it at that. The line began to grow, and he received the next customer. The two of them were with customers for the remainder of their shift, which was fine with Derrick. It brought him closer to his meeting with Aaron and a resolution to the questions swimming in his head.

Derrick was fidgeting again while Mr. Lauder locked up the store; this time, he could feel it. Brian was eyeballing him, only adding to the discomfort.

"Can I tag along? I'm curious," Brian asked.

"Sorry, this is an adventure for one."

Brian shrugged. "Can't blame a guy for trying."

"Have a good evening, crew." Mr. Lauder announced, and the employees left the building.

Derrick noticed that Brian's vehicle was two away from his, so he had to endure the heckling for another few minutes.

They walked in silence for the next ten yards before Brian spoke again.

"You even have Penny curious."

"You told her?" Derrick asked.

"Yeah, she *is* my fiancée," he said. "From what she says, I need to tell her everything. But a mystery like this with a clue like *being guarded by a higher power*, must be explored."

"I thought you didn't believe me when I told you that," Derrick said, picking up his pace.

"Slow down, will ya?" Brian said. "Of course, I don't. I know you don't believe in that stuff, either. You have said so yourself when Breonna goes on with her God talk."

Brian was right. He had spoken ill of Breonna a few times behind her back about her belief in God and how she spoke of her religion freely. A sick feeling hit his stomach—guilt. "Well, maybe I don't think Breonna is so far off anymore."

"Don't tell me you've become a Jesus Freak too?"

Derrick stopped short of his car and lifted his fist.

It frightened Brian.

"Hey now," Brian took a step back, raising his hands in protection. "I didn't mean to upset you. Sorry. We've said this stuff about her before. I guess you two dating has put the lid on all the silly religion stuff now."

"I don't know anymore, Brian," Derrick said, releasing his clenched fist, fanning his hand. "But let's just keep Breonna out of it, okay?"

"Okay," Brian said with a shaky voice.

"And keep the God talk to a minimum," Derrick said, pointing his finger at Brian.

"Umm, okay? Is that what this is all about?"

"I told you already. You just didn't want to listen," Derrick said, unlocking his car. "Now I need to go. I'm taking tomorrow off. I'll talk to you on Friday."

Brian stuttered another good-bye, and Derrick pulled off without letting his car warm up. He just needed to get out of there. He needed to get to Aaron and learn about what he meant by Carter being an angel sent to protect him and to bring him closer to God.

The diner was dark, as expected. Only the kitchen and front counter lights were on. There wasn't anyone behind the counter. With his attention focused there, the click of the front door lock startled him. Aaron noticed Derrick jump and apologized.

"It's okay," Derrick laughed. "I nearly screamed like a little girl."

Aaron laughed. "Come on inside. I have a pot on, and I still have some cobbler warm from the day shift."

Derrick figured he'd have to tough through a cup of joe. *Who knows,* he thought. *Maybe I could grow to like it now that I know it was an angel drinking the stuff that night three years ago.* He smiled at the thought, still a little in shock, still a bit in disbelief. Mostly wanting the answers he was hoping to get.

"How's business?" Derrick was first to speak once they sat.

"It was a busy day, but not too crazy. We don't have a special on Wednesdays—Pop hasn't come up with one, so we put up whatever we have most of in stock. If it's yesterday's Fried Chicken, Mom had a Chicken Salad recipe she would make. We had it today, but it wasn't quite the same. You know?"

"Yeah. No one can make something quite like Mom," Derrick said, his memory going back to his mom's dinners when she made them. Even a PB&J sandwich tasted different when he made it.

"Would you like some cobbler?" Aaron said, stepping behind the counter and washing his hands.

"Definitely," Derrick said, remembering his first encounter with it.

Aaron took a couple of healthy portions of cobbler out of the warmer and placed them into ramekins. He looked a bit nervous as he reached for the scooper.

"You okay?" Derrick asked.

"I'm going to do my best to make these the way Deborah made them," Aaron said, gently placing the scoop of ice cream into each dish. "The first time she portioned it for me, she tipped her hand to the secret ingredient of nutmeg." He picked up the shaker and looked at it. "I've never been able to nail the final mixture. There was just something she did that made it pop." Aaron gently tapped the nutmeg can with his hand over each dish. "All my years as a food critic and exploring food, and Aaron Stephenson can't duplicate a simple cobbler."

Aaron placed a spoon in each bowl and handed one to Derrick and placed the other in front of the empty seat beside him. As he walked around the counter, he grabbed a couple of cups of coffee and spoons.

Aaron sat and handed Derrick a spoon. With a *cheers clink*, he lifted it and said, "Okay. Here goes nothing." Then they both dove into their dessert.

Yet again, Derrick was sent to another world. He didn't know what Deborah's dessert was supposed to taste like, but this was a home run in his book. For the next several minutes, neither said anything beyond making *yummy* noises.

Derrick figured Aaron might have come close to honoring his loved one's recipe.

With bowls empty and spoons clanking, both men sat back and sipped on their coffees. Derrick realized that he didn't mind coffee. Would he become a regular drinker of the stuff? Probably not, but if Breonna would sit and drink a cup, he would perhaps join her.

Derrick wondered which one would be the first to speak about the subject floating in the air. It was Aaron who broke the silence.

"I guess you have quite a few questions for me. I know I've left you hanging more than once, but before I get into it too much, I want you to understand that I'm here for you, okay?"

Derrick was hesitant, but with what Aaron had told him before, he felt safe with him. He agreed that he would hear him out and not get upset.

"First, do you have any questions for me?"

Derrick thought for a moment. With his current studies, he always needed to ensure there was sufficient proof of anything before taking any sudden action. Being a social worker caused him to skate a thin line. Making false accusations could get him in big trouble, just as not taking action on unsubstantiated truths could hurt someone in serious need.

"I don't want to sound skeptical. I mean, when you look at the man, his appearance doesn't scream heavenly being."

"Is it supposed to?"

Derrick thought about it and had to admit that it would make little sense if Carter looked the part. If he resembled pictures in books or scenes in some movies, his cover would be blown, and the people he was sent to help may not receive the help they needed. If he had been approached by an angel that was brightly adorned, it would've freaked him out. Any change he made in his life would've been out of fear, not out of a pure heart. But he never had the chance to get to know Carter. He left before they got to know each other. That brought his first question to mind.

"If he was sent to guide me, why did he leave?"

Aaron took a breath, and his eyes left Derrick's.

Derrick noticed, "What?"

"You already know the answer. Carter had put two and two together about who you were."

"What does who I am matter," Derrick said, but even he said it, his mind strayed back to the stairs in his childhood home—and his mom with the man in the hat. His mom and—Carter. "Wait. Why was Carter sent to my mom back then?"

"For the same reason he was sent to you," Aaron said carefully.

"But my mom *was* a Christian. She read her Bible all the time, and she took me to church when she could. She believed in God," Derrick said with a confident tone.

"I can't answer that, but as far as I know, if Carter is sent to someone, their soul is in danger. Just as he was sent to Deborah. Her soul was in danger of being lost. Through his actions and the Little Reminders he left, she was brought back into a relationship with God, saving her."

"What was my mom lost from? I don't understand. If she was lost, then why did she have to die so suddenly?" Derrick said, his tone raised.

"Derrick, please remember. I lost a loved one too. Deborah died as well."

"But Deborah wasn't your mother!" Derrick shouted, pointing at Aaron. He turned his back, folding his hands behind his neck.

The room went silent. Derrick felt guilty the moment the words left his mouth. He knew that he shouldn't have said them and that they must've cut Aaron deep. He didn't want to turn around to face him again.

Derrick took a deep breath. "I'm sorry," he said. "I didn't mean to disrespect your loved one."

"You didn't. I shouldn't compare my pain to yours. I agree it's unequal. And I apologize for that. I'm just trying to get the point across that we've both experienced loss, and with that loss, there's also joy in it because of Carter."

"So, my mom and Deborah were both visited by Carter, and before each of them died, he was able to lead them back to God?"

There was a delay in Aaron's response. Derrick was not sure how to take it. "He was able to lead them, right?"

"I'm confident that Deborah turned back to God before she passed away. I never got to speak to Deborah directly about it. She died in surgery. But Carter visited me after Deborah's funeral. If she hadn't turned back to God, then I don't think that visit would have taken place."

"What about my mom?"

"I can't speak about another person's soul. That's for God to know."

"Or Carter. So, he is here because he's genuinely assigned to me, or he's here because it's a guilt trip over losing my mom." Derrick's voice trembled.

"Think about what you just said," Aaron responded. "If it were a guilt trip, would he be MIA right now? No, if anything, he would be trying too hard to win you over. I think he's here on a genuine assignment for you."

"I see your point. Then where is he? Where is Carter?"

"I wish I knew," Aaron shrugged.

"When was the last time you saw him?"

Aaron turned his face turn away.

"Aaron. You do realize that through my studies, I'm taught to discern whether a person is being honest or not? I'm sensing you are either being untruthful, or your thinking about it." Derrick grinned, then waved Aaron on. "Out with it."

"It's Carter's job to direct you on a path to find God again. I have told you about the Little Reminders Deborah found. You have talked about the ones you have found. Those reminders have to get in those places somehow, right?"

"Yeah, I figured that much already. Carter placed Deborah's items and mine," Derrick said.

"Yes. He kinda had help on the last one of yours," Aaron admitted.

"What? You? Ahhhh," Derrick said, pointing his finger. "That was *you* sitting in that car across the street. "I thought I heard something that day."

"Yes. It was both of us. Carter was struggling even then. I was trying to get him back on track with his job here," Aaron said.

Derrick was confused why the man who was supposed to be helping him could be running away from him. It didn't make sense. It felt like Aaron was dancing around the real issue—or leading up to it.

"What aren't you telling me, Aaron?" Derrick asked. It was time to cut to the chase.

Aaron took another sip of coffee. His cup had been empty for three sips now. Another tell that this was going to be huge. Derrick re-situated himself in his seat because this was potentially bigger than Carter just being an angel sent to save his soul.

"You have already figured out that Carter knew your mom three years ago before she died and that he worked with her to bring her—"

"Aaron!" Derrick cut in.

"I'm getting there, Derrick. This needs to be said. Trust me, it's important. Just hear me out."

"Okay, continue. I'm sorry."

"It's fine. Just hear me out."

"You know Carter knew your mom. He was the angel working to give her the Little Reminders to bring her back to knowing God and saving her soul. But what you don't know about Carter is that he isn't like a normal angel. To put it simply, there are heavenly angels, and there are angels here on earth. And the angels that are here on earth are still angels but bear many human characteristics. One of those is emotions," Aaron stretched the last word, then paused. He looked to Derrick for a reaction. A light went on behind his eyes.

"Are you trying to tell me that an angel of God fell in love with my mother?"

"I'm afraid so."

"So, that's what has him so upset? That he got paired up with me?"

"No, it isn't *you*. He blames himself for your mom's death."

Derrick thought about it for a while. It wasn't too long ago that he blamed the man in the hat for his mom's death. He was the one his mom was arguing with not too long before she passed away. Why should it matter that the man had a name now?

"Isn't it his fault?" Derrick said. "If they hadn't been arguing, she may not have gotten into that accident."

"Was she driving?"

"No, my aunt was."

"Was your aunt at fault?"

"No."

"And most importantly, let me ask you this. How long after the argument was this accident?"

Derrick was silent. The reality hit him as he answered. "A couple of months."

"Then how could Carter be at fault for that accident?"

Derrick knew Aaron was right. The accident wasn't Carter's fault. It was just another teenage excuse. He had been mad at the world for the loss of his mom. The mystery man was just a scapegoat at the time.

"But why would God take my mom in such an awful way? Why couldn't she die peacefully, in surgery as Deborah did?"

Aaron laughed. "You think Deborah died peacefully? She may not have complained about it, but she was in pain. Maybe not scream your head off pain, but she had a tumor growing in her head. She had no clue what was happening to her, and the doctors were clueless. They had their hands tied with what they could do. Once they realized what she really had, it was too late.

"I know some would like the opportunity to be able to say good-bye, but to either face a drawn-out death like Deborah had, or to have a quick death as your mom had with her accident—I don't know about you, but I think I'd prefer to check out like your mom. Your mom is with Christ now, in Heaven. No pain, not having to deal with the craziness of the world, no bills to pay, no more listening to the complaints of those wanting more. She got it in the blink of an eye and not with the long-drawn-out sentence like my DeeDee had. If I'm being honest, I think you had it lucky."

Derrick smiled. He had to admit, Aaron had a point. If he did have a wish for his mom, it was to not suffer in death. And that was most definitely answered. A bit sooner than he anticipated, but answered. "I just wish it wasn't so soon."

"But God had a plan through it all, Derrick. You just need to find it." Aaron said, placing his hand on Derrick's shoulder. "And if you mention a word to Pop that I called my fiancée, *DeeDee*, you'll be next Wednesday's special."

"Gotcha," Derrick said with a thumbs up.

Chapter
Seventeen

Derrick thanked the waitress for his pastry and coffee. He briefly conversed with Gary who was sitting at his usual spot, spouting off about another home team loss. But when Derrick reached for the door, something that Carter said echoed in his mind—*Everyone has a story*. Derrick looked back at Gary, suddenly wondering what his story was. Gary wore a Gulf War veteran's cap, decorated with multiple pins. He was curious what each of those pins meant.

When the bell to Derrick's exit didn't sound, Gary turned in his direction. "Everything okay, son?" Gary asked.

Derrick turned and walked back to his table. "May I ask you a couple of questions, Gary?"

Gary looked a bit confused at first. A kid who had up until now only exchanged box scores or simple pleasantries was now two feet from him and wanted to engage in actual conversation. "Um, yeah, sure. Have a seat," he said, gesturing to the seat across from him.

"Thank you, sir. I won't take too much of your time. I need to get to class, but I'd like to know more about you. It seems we pass each other every day and only know each other's first names. I see your hat, and I feel I do you an injustice only to say, *Thank you for your service*, without actually knowing what that service was."

Gary's eyes began to tear up. Derrick wasn't sure if that was a good thing or bad. He may have opened a wound for him. He had heard of shell shock and PTSD. He now wished he had thought his approach through before making it. Perhaps this was a bad idea.

"Son," Gary began, "you're the first person who has wanted to know anything about my experiences in Afghanistan and Iraq." Gary nodded from Derrick's wide-eyed expression. "Yes, I was in both countries. Heh, more than once. I did six tours. Six, over eight years before I was wounded, and Uncle Sam decided that was enough for me."

"Wounded?"

"Yeah. Shot in the upper hip. You wouldn't know it because you've never seen me walk, but I have a decent hobble. Now that I'm older, it affects me more."

"Wow. I didn't know."

"How could you?"

Derrick looked up at the clock on the wall and frowned. "Gary, I really want to hear more. One morning, I'll come in when I don't have to rush off, and maybe you would be willing to talk about it?"

Gary smiled. "I would be honored."

"Great." Derrick headed to the door and quickly spun around and picked up his pastry. "Almost forgot," he said with a grin.

Derrick left the restaurant a little more educated about a man he passed every day and took for granted; another story he learned a little more about. He was sure it was filled with the happiness and sadness that Carter told him about. With the veteran sitting alone, Derrick wondered if there was ever a Mrs. Gary. That was a subject he wanted to explore, and it reminded him of another love, the love that Carter potentially had for his mom. He wondered how she felt about him. Was Carter's raised voice that night a desperate plea over unreciprocated emotions, or was it over the realization that they couldn't be together and it was the end of a romance that could never be? He needed to find Carter to get answers.

Derrick was beginning to discover that his studies were not just applicable to kids and teens. He found that even adults struggle with discovering who they are. It was something he should have figured out by now. He was still on a path of learning who he was in his own life. In just the past couple of weeks, he learned things about himself and his past that had turned his world upside down. What he did with this infor-mation would set the course of his future. He had courses where he studied these pivotal points. He had written papers on them and scored highly. But now he was living it. How would the head knowledge convert to life experience? Only time would tell.

Derrick walked down the stairs after his final class of the day feeling more relaxed—no running today, no dodging freshman. Maybe he had grown up over the past few weeks. Perhaps panic was what kept him on edge all the time. He had done some thinking the last couple of days. He thought of the day he saw Carter sitting in the park. He thought of him relaxing with a book in a library. He seemed not to have a care in the world. What gave a person that much peace? Putting the angelic being aside, Aaron said Carter experienced human emotion, so there must be opportunities for him to experience anxiety, but up until now, Carter seemed to have none. What if the peace he had was from the source inside him? What if the peace he had came from God?

The list of questions he need Carter to answer continued to pile up. But the peace, Derrick thought, could begin now—that was a conscience self-choice. So, no panicking. He would take his time and not worry about getting to work on time. He danced through students and into the garage. His car started and heated up with no issues, and he moved through traffic with ease. No busy intersections or troublesome officers with bad attitudes disturbed his calm. He pulled up to the bookstore with twenty minutes to spare, a new record.

"Huh," Derrick said aloud. He sat enjoying his car's warmth, a cold front had blown through the day before. He wasn't looking forward to the walk to the building. He looked to the back seat and grabbed his jacket. A clunking sound drew his attention to the floorboard. It was his mother's Bible. It had been resting on his jacket. He looked up and around the parking lot for Aaron or Carter, then remembered he had just pulled up.

With time available, Derrick picked up the Bible and thumbed through it, landing on another bookmark in Second Corinthians.

"Therefore, if anyone is in Christ, he is a new creation; old things have passed away; behold, all things have become new."

"A new creation," Derrick said aloud. "That would definitely be a good story to tell."

He thought of Aaron and Deborah's story, of how God directed them together, and how their Little Reminders helped save Deborah. Even Aaron had his story of being led back to God through what Carter had done. His thoughts drifted back to Gary. Did he have a story, a *God-incidence*, as Aaron put it? He wondered, did everyone have an angel as he did? And was he and the ones around him the only ones they could impact?

"Lord, if you're really there, I need to know. People keep telling me you are and that you've sent someone to show me you are. I'm just not so sure. Am I *that* important to you? Do you really care about more than just the big picture? I'm just one man. I don't see how I can matter so much. But if you do care, thank you."

Derrick glanced at his watch and realized he only had two minutes to clock in. He gritted his teeth, stepped out into the cold, and somehow made it from his vehicle to the time clock with a few seconds to spare. He wiped his brow, grabbed a water bottle from the employee lounge, and downed it before heading up to the register.

"I have a question for you, Derrick. Rather a favor," Breonna said as she approached him. He had finally broken from the register to build a couple of new release displays. Her face was more serious than normal. Her smile wasn't carrying its usual sparkle. If he didn't know better, he would say there was a hint of fear behind it. *This doesn't look good.*

"Sure, Breonna. What do you need?" Derrick asked. He wished he had been heading to the register, then perhaps he could have been given a warning, or at least a hint of what was about to come from Brian.

"What are Sundays like?" Breonna asked, her eyes everywhere but meeting his.

"I usually sleep until my eyes pop open. But the week before last, I went to the church I grew up in." With those words, Breonna's head jerked up, and her eyes met his.

"And," she probed.

"And I was okay with it, but at the time, I just felt it wasn't for me."

"Oh," Breonna said, her eyes turning back to the floor.

"But," Derrick continued, "last week, I woke up and felt the pull to get out of bed. But I didn't. I ignored it. In fact, I forced it down. And I tell you, I regretted it. I was practically ill the entire day. I can't explain it. I just felt off."

Breonna poked his arm. "It's called guilt."

"Guilt? Naww." Derrick said. "What guilt?"

"Think about it. You went to church, and you experienced something. Then the next week, you felt the urge to go but didn't. The urge was your spirit pulling you back."

"I don't understand that. My spirit?"

"It's what's inside you that craves the good. You know, when you were there, and you had those moments where it felt right? That God was speaking to you. It may have been fleeting, but there were moments where God got through."

Derrick thought back, and he did remember moments during the music where it was like a warm blanket had been wrapped around him. And during the preaching, at times it felt like the pastor was speaking directly and only to him.

"Ha," Breonna said. "I can see it in your eyes. You remember."

"Yeah, so what if I do?"

"That was the pull you felt the Sunday you didn't go. Your

spirit longed for those feelings again, and it knew where to get it, so it was trying to get you up to go where it needed you to go."

"Really?"

"If you were hungry for food and you had only eaten at the Burger King over on Calhaven. Now, your mind and stomach only knew of that BK, then where do you think both would be longing to go?" Breonna tapped Derrick's stomach, then looked up at him with raised her eyebrows.

"I see," Derrick said, half smiling.

"Same with your spirit. It longs for food too. For you, it only has experience with the church you went to last week, so the pull was to go back. And when you didn't go, your body felt the guilt of not obeying the spiritual pull."

"Is this what you wanted to talk to me about? The condition of my spiritual pull?"

Breonna smiled. "Kinda. I wanted to invite you to my church on Sunday. I was concerned that maybe you had never been to church."

"Naw, I grew up going to church with my mom. But then life got too busy, and after my mom passed…" Derrick didn't complete the sentence. He let it stand on its own.

"I understand. I'm sorry." Breonna said. She stayed silent for a moment, then took a breath and softly asked. "Would you consider attending with me and my family?"

"Your family?"

"Well, since I have my own car, it would be me and my brother, but it's my family's church."

"Ahh, okay." Derrick was nervous about agreeing to go, but he remembered wanting to experiment with churches, even wondering about Breonna's church. This was his opportunity.

And if there were to be a future with her, he needed to explore her belief in God.

"You know, Breonna, yes. I'd love to go with you. I have been thinking about it recently, and I know I need to get back on track."

Throughout the rest of their shift, they discussed the details. He would meet her at Calhaven Baptist Church. It happened to be close to the school, which was not too far from her home. He was glad it was the same denomination he was accustomed to. Maybe it would at least be a little less awkward than if it were a completely different demonination. By the end of their shift, plans to attend her church were set—and so was another date for Saturday afternoon and maybe a Spaghetti Sub to complete the day.

Chapter
Eighteen

Derrick pulled into the church parking lot. His heart attempted to escape his chest, but he explained that if he had to go through this experience, so did it. He parked in a spot as close to an exit as possible. If he needed to make a quick exit, he was going to be able to get in his car and escape with no hindrances whatsoever. Once he was satisfied, he messaged Breonna he had arrived and began his trek toward the entrance to the building.

The church looked much like Faith Community, but about fifty years newer. This church's stucco finish bore a fresh coat of paint and was free of age-old cracks and water stains that had etched their way through and tattooed themselves into Faith Community's character. There were three men at the doors compared to the two he saw at FCC. Each bore bright-colored ties and smiles and seemed to get in line to greet him. It almost felt as if he were expected.

"Good morning, sir. I'm Adam. It's good to have you with us," he said with a firm handshake.

"Yes, it's a pleasure to meet you. I'm Jonathan," said another.

The third was the most uptight, nearly saluting when giving his greeting, "Pleasure to meet you, sir. I'm Kendall."

Johnathan nearly fell over with laughter. Adam shook his head, "You will have to forgive our friend. It's his first week as a greeter. He's a bit anxious."

Derrick knew about trying too hard to fit in. "It's alright. I understand about overcompensating. I'm a social worker and see it all the time."

"A social worker?" Adam said with genuine interest on his face. "I'll have to get with you on that one," he said. "That type of work is interesting."

"Sure, we can talk later, and you can pick my brain," Derrick said with a grin.

"Are you new this week?" The third infantry soldier said in a firm tone. Derrick smiled at his attempt. He was trying.

"Yes, sir, I am. But I'm meeting someone. Breonna Greene?"

"Ah, yes. The Greene family. I know them well," Adam said. "They should be coming in soon. Sunday School is still in session. You can come in and be seated if you'd like."

Johnathan handed Derrick a bulletin, and he walked into the sanctuary. It was a bit larger than Faith Community. There were several more rows of pews, and on the wall behind the stage was an electronic screen rotating through announcements: *Thanksgiving Offering Today $2000 goal; Men's Breakfast December 5th; Christmas Caroling December 16th.* The stage itself was near twice the size of his church and bore instruments other than just a piano.

This should be interesting. Derrick couldn't remember hearing anything other than a piano or organ while singing worship music during a church service. He wasn't sure what to expect.

An older couple sitting on the right of the sanctuary gave

him a curious look but then smiled and politely waved. The family on the left extended the same greeting. Only they pulled their kids in tighter, all while delivering the *we trust you; we just don't believe you are trustworthy* grin. Derrick just grinned, hoping to relieve their—and his—anxiety.

Derrick for a moment wished Breonna's parents were in the sanctuary. Then he wouldn't have to pace, wondering what the seating arrangement was like here. He had no desire to stand out by sitting in *someone's spot*. So he paced. After his second pass, he heard a bell tone that sounded like the school bell ending a period. Then, a handful at a time, groups of people began to trickle into the sanctuary.

Two men walked down the aisle, and Derrick stopped one of them. "Sorry, sir. Have you seen Breonna Greene or her family?"

"Yes, they're in their Sunday School class. They should be on their way. Sorry, I need to get back to the sound system and prepare for the Live Stream."

"Sure, sorry. Thanks for your help," Derrick said, excusing the young man.

Derrick watched the man head back to the sound booth. He chuckled and looked around. Children were running and screaming, a few adults and elderly folk were trickling in from the back, being greeted by Adam and Johnathan, spots were being filled, and some spots were *not* being filled. *Ten to one,* Derrick thought, *one of those empties was reserved for Breonna and her family.*

Derrick reached the back of the aisle and turned around. From the entry to the left of the stage, a young man who bore a striking resemblance to a tardy car thief, came through the door. He was followed by the most beautiful creature ever to grace the hall of Calhaven Baptist Church. He had never seen her in anything but jeans or slacks, but a dress certainly became her.

"Good morning, Derrick," Breonna said, keeping her distance. *Church distance*, he figured. *Or more likely parental distance. Dad must be in the vicinity.*

"Hey, Bree," Derrick said without thinking. She blushed at the sudden use of a nickname.

"Did you have any trouble finding the place?"

"Not at all. The school is around the corner. I pass by here now and then when traffic is backed up on the main road." Derrick looked around for the inevitable. "Where are your parents?"

"They're coming. We don't attend the same class. They're in another part of the building."

"Oh, okay," Derrick said. A few minutes reprieve. That didn't stop his heart from wanting to pierce through his chest. He looked around. "Where do we sit?"

"Over here," Breonna said, pointing back a couple of rows.

As they sat, Breonna kept a person's distance between them. He wondered if her dad had a talk with her before this meeting took place. He could imagine it, *'Now, Breonna, the church is not a club where you meet people. If you bring him, you must be respectable.'* Derrick laughed aloud at the thought.

"What?" Breonna asked.

"Nothing," Derrick said, trying to tuck his smile away. "So, you've been attending here for a while then?"

"Since I can remember," she said. "And I turn twenty-one in December."

Great, Derrick thought. The daggers will be out in full force. Now everyone has a stake in being this girl's protector.

He glanced subtly around to see who could be eyeing him now. An elderly couple to his back right had a silly grin, and another just in front to the right glanced once or twice and gave the stink eye. Other than that, no one paid much attention—yet.

"Breonna," came an authoritative, almost militant voice. It sent needles up Derrick's spine that pinned him to his pew. It took Breonna's elbow to unstick him. He stood and was amazed that the man who stood before him was a good three inches shorter than he was. It nearly made him laugh.

"Derrick," Breonna said. "This is my father. You'll meet mom later. She's up in the choir."

Mr. Greene extended his hand and gave Derrick's much larger hand a firm handshake. His size was nothing to be ridiculed. This man had power. "Good to meet you, Derrick. I've heard a lot about you. Psychology student?"

"Yes, sir. I look to be a social worker."

"Impressive," Mr. Greene said. "That must be a difficult field."

"Yes, sir. I want to be able to help kids who have challenges overcome them. Difficulties like I had growing up."

"Yes, Breonna has told us about your mother," Mr. Green said, placing his hand on Breonna's shoulder. "Sorry for your loss, son."

"Thank you, Mr. Greene. It was a few years ago. I'm getting over it and moving on with my life, getting on with school, and doing what I can to help others."

"And where does my daughter fit into this?"

"Sir?" Derrick said, shocked at such a blunt question.

"Daddy!" Breonna said, elbowing him in the side.

"What?" Mr. Green said. "I'm just—"

This time it was a daughterly punch to the gut. "Really?"

Mr. Greene laughed. "Okay, okay," he said.

"Pleasure to meet you, Derrick. I better take my seat before I end up with a ruptured spleen."

Mr. Greene sat a row up and to the end of the aisle while Breonna and Derrick sat in their original seats, still a person-width apart. Derrick figured this was not a date, so it was understandable. Church was church. He remembered hearing his mom say, *When you're at church, you are there for God and not hanky panky.* She said that after seeing a deacon and his new girlfriend in each other's arms during a service.

As the sanctuary began to fill, Derrick picked up on a couple of obvious differences between this church and his— the most obvious was the stage for the pastor and choir instead of a small platform. Then there was an entire sound system instead of a single mic stand for the preacher. Not that his pastor needed a sound system. He was loud enough for the smaller room. This sanctuary had two speakers in the front corners, and it had two more hanging from the ceiling near the center of the stage. Not that ambiance would sway him to choose this over that; it was one of those things he noticed. It was just different.

As the service started, the sounds began to drown him. It was a much different experience than Faith Community. The music was beautiful, and the words had meaning, but it felt overwhelming for some reason. He remembered the feelings while singing the praise and worship songs at Faith Community. He remembered the tugging he felt last Sunday when he didn't attend service. It wasn't that he didn't feel God's presence, it just felt like he was in someone else's pool. Yes, he felt God speaking to him through the pastor's message, and he felt better walking out than walking in. But he already knew where he would be next week. It wasn't about the flash; it was about the presence of the Lord. And Faith Community is where Derrick felt he needed to be to get his heart back on track with God. He just prayed that Breonna would understand.

Chapter

Nineteen

Nearly a week had passed, and Derrick had not been able to find Carter. When he wasn't at work or with Breonna, he spent his evenings searching parks and smaller libraries for any sign of him. He spoke to librarian after librarian. Most knew Carter by description and had seen him once or twice, but not recently. The central library was the only one with a current sighting, so he went to that location on his day off to study and complete a paper on Leadership Mannerisms. His professor for this class was much more laid back than Professor Adkins. He didn't scare the junk out of him.

"We're getting ready to close, sir," the library clerk reminded Derrick. He looked at his laptop clock. It showed it was nearing 10:00—another day without a Carter sighting.

"Thank you, Marianne," Derrick said. "Any sign of my friend?"

"No, I'm sorry. I kept my eyes out, too. So did the other clerks. We all love Carter around here. He knows almost as much as we do," she said with a caring laugh. "I sure hope you find him. When you do, tell him we miss him."

"I will," Derrick said, putting his computer away. "Maybe he sees me and stays away."

"Don't say that," Marianne said with furrowed brows. "I know you guys had a disagreement, but if I know Carter, he won't stay upset long. It's not like him to get emotional like that."

"That's what people keep telling me," Derrick said, exhaling, toeing a chair leg. "Well, I better let you close up. I'm sure you want to get home."

Marianne led him to the door and locked it behind him. The myriad of sidewalk sleepers wasn't as plentiful as it had been. He was grateful. It was in the forties, and the breeze made it feel chillier than that. Only a few were taking shelter against the building, but they were among the experienced and well-sheltered with makeshift dwellings. Law enforcement wasn't around. He guessed they let them be as they seemed to keep to themselves. It amazed Derrick how much someone could get used.

The chill urged him on to the warmth of his car. He rounded the corner and saw a shadowed figure standing near his vehicle. Derrick stopped, as did his heart, until he realized the figure bore a resemblance to a long-sought-after lover of literature.

"You know, I'm usually the one watching and waiting," the familiar figure called out.

"That can get kinda creepy, old man," Derrick said.

"You don't know the half of it. And you'd be surprised to know how old I am, Derrick."

"Given the past two weeks, probably not," Derrick replied as he walked up to his car door across from where Carter stood.

Carter laughed. "I supposed not. Gabriel can be mysterious, but he has a tendency to be straightforward."

"Who?"

"Ahh. Never mind. Guess he's only gotten hold of Aaron. But Aaron has gotten to you. And that's pretty much the same thing," Carter said, stroking his stubble.

"I've been looking for you everywhere."

"Yes, I know. And I've been watching you looking for me. You need to drive more carefully. First, you almost get into an accident. Then the ticket? *Tsk. Tsk. Tsk.* My dear Derrick."

Derrick just shook his head. "First of all, I didn't get a ticket. Second, why do you keep running from me? I just want to talk. We *need* to talk."

"I didn't have anything to say then," Carter replied.

"And you do now?"

"Perhaps."

Derrick let the half answer hang in the air. He took a deep breath and looked at his watch. "I know you like coffee. You want to get a cup somewhere?"

"I think it's time for us to clear the air and get back on track. There are things to do and little time to do them," Carter said, opening his door. "There is a place around the block that serves a fabulous mocha. I never used to touch the stuff, but one of the gentlemen here suggested it, and now I can't stop drinking it."

Derrick laughed. "Sounds great. I think I know the place. It's an all-nighter for college students who need to study and stay awake."

"Yes. I believe that's the place. There are quite a few computer connection stations and some modern types of music. Not my style, but I can stomach it if the coffee is good enough."

Carter asked him about classes on their way, and Derrick explained his recent windfall with Professor Adkins.

"You know it was you who inspired our connection?" Derrick said.

"Is that right?"

"You talked about everyone having their own story; that some have good stories, and some have not so good stories. But each of our stories needs to be read."

"Yes, I did say that. Everyone has a story to tell," Carter beamed.

"Well, before that memory came back to me, I was in the library getting my midterm printed out for my most difficult professor. The librarian, go figure, mentioned that I should take it easy and not give Professor Atkins a difficult time. She didn't say why. She just left off with those words.

"My first attempt to talk with him, I looked like an idiot. But I think making a fool of myself opened the door later, because it put my name on his lips. My second approach, he knew who I was. We talked and realized we had things in common, and he began to value my work. He even submitted my midterm to a literary magazine."

"Impressive."

"I wouldn't have made the approach if you had not given me that speech. It reminded me that everyone is human. That even though we see those that appear high and lofty, they have souls too. They can be hurt and have hurts. While I don't fully know what his is, I think his past is similar to mine."

"What gave you that impression?"

"He praised my writing based on study alone."

"And of course, it's not," Carter said knowingly.

"Right. I explained that I had lived most of what I had written. That's when he gave me the look," Derrick said, trying to deliver the look to Carter.

"Ah, the blended look of being impressed and kindred spirit—he had been there," Carter nodded.

"That's what I believe, yes. He didn't use words, but I feel it in my heart."

"Well done, Derrick."

"Thank you," Derrick said, feeling a bit more qualified being thanked by someone outside the college community for the experience he had lived.

Derrick pulled into the lot and shut off the engine. "Do you really want to go in and have coffee?"

Carter looked up at the bright lights, then back to Derrick. "No, not really."

Derrick took a deep breath and held it, then exhaled. It was now or never. "I know what happened. Well, I don't know all that happened. But I have a pretty good idea. It took me a while to figure it out. But it's what makes sense. I just don't know how the story ended, and that's the blank I need filled in. Only you have that answer."

"I'm fairly sure I know what your concern is, Derrick. And I apologize for putting you through this. I'm sorry I couldn't get over myself sooner and come to you. Yes, I fell in love with your mother. It was something that never should have happened. I'm still not sure how it happened. Your mom *was* an amazing person. That's part of it. But I'm an angel of the Lord. I should have known better."

"What was the disagreement about that night? I heard you arguing?" Derrick asked.

Carter was silent. Derrick tried to figure out if it was guilt or if he was just trying to remember. His face didn't show either.

"Your mother had terminal cancer. She had maybe a year at most to live."

Derrick shook his head, "Naw. Naw, Carter. She would've told me. She wasn't seeing a doctor."

"Where do you think she was coming from when she got into the accident, and why was your aunt driving and not your mom?

"Our fight was because she said she wanted to give up. She said the chemo was too much to go through for, *Maybe one or two years more.* She said she would rather live one halfway good year with you and me than go through it sick, clouded, and miserable. So we argued. I said something I shouldn't have, and I left."

Carter began to tear up. "A month went by, and the next thing I know, she was killed in a car accident. I never had the opportunity to apologize. More than that, I never had the opportunity to complete my mission of leaving the final reminders I was assigned to leave her."

Derrick wiped his tears with his sleeve. He had no idea of her condition. If anything, she had seemed happier leading up to her passing—up until that night. Then it occurred to him that her happiness could have come from meeting someone. In spite of her illness, she had fallen in love. He wondered what Carter said to her that could have been so damaging to them both. By the tears in Carter's eyes, his regrets were still like a millstone. He had no intention of pushing him back over the edge.

"I had no idea, Carter. Of her illness or her involvement with you. I wish I had known about both. I don't know why the both of you kept it hidden. I was eighteen years old."

"Your mom was about to tell you. It was part of what we argued about. I can't tell you why she kept it a secret. But the good thing was it looked like she kept going to chemotherapy.

That's where she was coming home from. So, she was trying to stay around a bit longer for you."

"Why didn't you ever come to me?"

"You weren't my assignment. She was."

Derrick swallowed hard, knowing he had to ask the next question.

"Did you complete your assignment, Carter?'

Carter was silent. He stared out the windshield. The glow from the neon sign glistened off of the tears rolling down his cheek.

"I believe so," Carter said. "I'm hardly ever present when those I'm sent to make their choice to come back to God. That's usually a personal encounter in prayer. I've had a few ask me to pray with them, but not many."

Derrick was silent. Carter's answer would have to suffice. He did his best. It wasn't like he had pushed her away from God. He gave her love that she hadn't seen for a long time. Derrick was grateful for what Carter had brought to his mom's life. And regardless of the secrecy, it was something he had to live with. He still struggled with Carter being an angelic being and his mom being—his mom.

"So, what's next?" Derrick asked.

"You tell me, Derrick? Where do you feel *you* are at with the Lord right now?"

Chapter
Twenty

Carter had given Derrick a lot to think about. Why he couldn't answer Carter's question, he didn't know. His blank stare seemed to disappoint Carter, but Derrick explained that he was confused. He had spent three weeks in three different spiritual experiences and was unsure what was going on inside his heart and head. He told Carter he just needed more time. Carter nodded with an accepting pout, then reminded him that waiting wasn't always wise. He reminded him of how quickly a life can be taken, and after that, it was too late.

Derrick replied that he understood but felt that God was guiding him and wanted him to feel certain before turning over that leaf. To which Carter again pout-nodded.

"Just don't wait too long. I wouldn't want to mourn over your soul as well," Carter said before he left his car, and walked toward the library. He refused to go anywhere else.

Derrick planned to spend the morning with Gary. His shift

didn't start until eleven, so he woke up early and headed to the taco shop.

Like clockwork, Gary was in his chair, nursing his coffee and whatever breakfast he had eaten. They spoke of Gary's service to his country, all six tours, each having its own adventures. Gary bore the scars of injury, friends gone, and loves lost. A novel could be written based on his life.

It happened that Gary was still married, and that his wife lived in a nursing home not too far from the taco house. Every morning, he came there and waited until visiting hours opened at nine. His eyes locked with Derrick's as he talked about never giving up on his wife through the good and the bad.

"In life you will experience highs and lows. You will go through hell and back, son. There will be days that you will look at her and wonder why in the world you married that woman. Then there will be days when you feel like life couldn't get any better. It's called marriage. Marriage is a choice. It's not a coat you buy, and when you don't like it anymore, you return it or toss it in the trash. No. You stick it out. What God has brought together, let not man separate."

Derrick nodded. "I hope to find a woman that makes me that happy." Derrick's face must have slipped into thoughts of Breonna because the older man beamed.

"Ahh," Gary pointed. "That look on your face. Who is she?"

"We just started dating," Derrick said, not even trying to hide it anymore. "I can't know that depth of affection yet."

"Nonsense, Derrick." Gary leaned into him. "When the heart knows, it knows."

Derrick shook his head. "It's complicated."

"Well, I hope it gets uncomplicated before she slips away."

Derrick nodded, extending his hand. "It was a pleasure having this time with you, Gary. I need to be heading off. Work beckons."

Gary gripped the outstretched hand. "The pleasure was mine. Again, thank you for taking an interest in my past. It was good to talk about it again. Each time I do, a bit of its pain is released. I appreciate you."

Derrick accepted the compliment with a glad heart. He hadn't considered that just listening to his story would have such an effect. Most of what he was learning through schooling was aimed at the younger generation. He hadn't considered it might be applicable for colleagues or those who were his senior. He just found a topic for his Diversity and Human Development paper.

Exiting the restaurant, it was his turn to be hidden. He didn't want to face Carter without having an answer to his question. He just wanted to get to work unseen—not that a bookshelf or a counter could hide him from Carter Jennings. He had been across from him at his job before. Derrick's radar was on high alert. He had yet to talk to Breonna about his friend, even though they had spent quite a bit of time together away from work when he wasn't scouring the city. How would he explain Carter anyhow? Out of everyone, Breonna would most likely believe in angels, but he couldn't take that risk.

Derrick finished his second cart of returns for the evening and started his trek back to the front. He peeked around the corner in search of tweed. This must have made him look suspicious, because he heard the familiar melt-your-heart-to-a-puddle laugh.

"What in the world are you doing, silly?" Breonna asked, coming down the aisle behind him.

Busted. What could he say? "Looking for someone," Derrick responded, but it sounded more like a question than an answer.

"That doesn't sound too promising. Do you owe them money or something?"

Derrick exhaled and then smiled. "No, it's nothing like that. I just don't want to see them right now."

"Who might this them be? A crazy ex, maybe?"

"Bree?"

"What? You're the one who is being evasive," Breonna said, half-joking, half-serious.

"It's not a female if that makes you feel better," Derrick said, placing his hand on her shoulder. "It's just a friend I don't want to see right now."

"Did you—"

"Please, Breonna," Derrick interrupted. "I don't want to talk about it right now. Please respect that."

"Okay," she said in a soft voice.

Derrick could see that she was hurt but respected his stance.

"I need to check my section and see if there are any customers," she said. "I'll talk to you later."

Derrick watched her walk away, feeling remorse for talking to her as he did. All she ever did was try to help him, and all he ever seemed to do was snuff her attempts. It was a wonder she hadn't walked away yet. He wondered how many more chances he had before she did just that.

With the concern over his love life, he had lost focus on why he was sneaking peeks like a private eye in the spy novels Breonna was so fond of telling him about. He edged his neck around the corner, and when he was sure the coast was clear, he headed back to the register with his cart.

Carter didn't make an appearance that shift—at least not that he knew of. From his own admission, he had been watching. How he did this was beyond him. For all Derrick knew, he could make himself invisible and sit in a corner and just watch. Just the thought sent shivers down his spine. But according to Aaron, Carter wasn't like other angels. He was earthbound and limited to what he could and couldn't do.

After his shift ended, Derrick sat in the coffee house. Breonna got off an hour later. He was hoping she would see him there and stop in. That was Plan A. Plan B was to meet her in the parking lot. Either plan included public groveling, then hopefully a meal afterward. Breonna had taken a liking to Davies Deli. They had been there twice that week. Derrick had to admit, Pop did have a good thing going. Breonna fell in love with the Chicken Caesar Salad Sub. But she had yet to try the Spaghetti Sub. It so happened it was that day's sub. Maybe today would be the day.

The clock on the wall told Derrick it was ten after four. Breonna should be heading his way any second. The knot in his throat tightened as the second hand ticked away. Then he saw her dark hair come into view. Her head almost didn't turn, but as if she had an internal radar on him, she stopped walking and looked his way. A smile almost reached her face but faded. *Was that a good or bad sign?*

Breonna entered the shop and walked up to his table. "I didn't think you cared for coffee."

"It grows on you," Derrick said.

"What are you doing in here," she asked after a heavy breath, her eyebrows raised.

"Waiting for you."

"I have somewhere I need to be," Breonna said.

"Really? Where?"

Breonna's face went blank. He could tell she wasn't ready to be challenged. Her eyes darted everywhere but on his, and they began to tear up.

"Bree. I'm sorry. I didn't mean to snap at you. I apologize for hurting your feelings. Please forgive me."

Derrick looked to the ground. Breonna looked back up at him, her eyes a bit confused. He was a little stunned at his choice of words himself. But they had been said. It wasn't that he didn't mean them. He did. But where they came from, he couldn't say.

"I forgive you, Derrick," Breonna said. "It wasn't that big of a deal. I just want you to know that you can be open with me. I want you to feel safe with me."

"I know," Derrick said. It was his turn to swallow. "I just need time. It's hard for me to be open, much less feel completely safe. I've never been in this situation before. I want you to know that I'm not going anywhere. I may be a jerk at times, but please know it's not you. I'm going through some things right now. I wish I could tell you, but it's something I need to face alone right now. I need you to trust me."

Breonna nodded, brushing away a tear. "Just promise me that if it gets too tough, you'll talk to someone." Breonna smiled through her tears. "Promise?"

"Breonna," Derrick said, taking her hand, then kissing it, "I promise. And if it gives you any comfort, I'm on this road with others, and we're surrounded in prayer. I'm not strug-gling—I'm just finding the answer I need."

"So, this is spiritual?" Breonna asked, sitting across from him.

"You could say that," Derrick said.

"Can I help?"

Derrick thought about telling her everything, but the *crazy Derrick* feeling crept up and convinced him it was best to hold off. "Not right now. I think this battle is best for me to fight alone. At least for now. You can pray, though."

Breonna beamed. "That I can most certainly do."

Derrick took a breath and looked at the clock that was still ticking his life away. "You hungry?"

"I'm famished," Breonna said. "But!" she said almost at a shout, "I will not, *will* not, eat a Spaghetti Sub. I will not do it for you, bub. I won't eat it with a grub. I won't eat it with a cub."

"Seriously, Bree?" Derrick said, the air deflating from his balloon.

Breonna laughed, wiping the dew from her cheeks and standing. She reached out her hand, and Derrick took it. "C'mon. Let's go eat."

Chapter
Twenty-One

Pop was happy to see his *two favorite customers* back for another meal. Jasmine was giving Erica a run for her money; two teas were already on the counter next to Aaron with sweetener and lemon by the time Derrick and Breonna sat. Jasmine leaned into them as they sat, "Meatloaf and Caesar Salad?" she asked.

Derrick and Breonna nodded without a second thought. Aaron leaned over. "Benefit of knowing the owner," he whispered with a wink and went back to typing on his computer. They both laughed, sipping their tea.

Aaron knew about Carter's visit with Derrick, and that they had talked about the details of his mom's relationship with Carter. But Derrick didn't reveal the challenges he was facing. He felt that it was something he had to deal with on his own. He didn't need an extra voice in his ear and the pressure that would come with it. Carter's voice alone was enough.

"So, how does it feel to be on break?" Aaron asked, not looking up from his computer screen.

"Great," the two students responded in unison, then laughed.

"Gonna need this one," Breonna said. "Just seeing what the human body goes through gives you an appreciation for it."

"I can somewhat understand," Aaron said. He stopped typing and sat back. "We did a piece on nursing about a year ago. Hospitals were considering cutting staff just before the pandemic broke out. Then the nurses were suddenly needed, and they were sure glad they kept them around. The piece centered around the behind-the-scenes work nurses do that the gen-pub doesn't get to see. That list is quite extensive. The hours they put in, the situations they deal with day in and day out, not to mention the lack of appreciation. I applaud you, Breonna. You're a strong and amazing person for selecting such a field as a career. May God bless you in it."

"Thanks, Aaron. I appreciate that. True, it's not always easy. And I'm still in school. But we're moving into field training soon. It can get overwhelming."

"I've spent my share of time around nurses. They don't get the appreciation they deserve. So, I'm giving you appreciation now. Remember it when you reach the top," Aaron said, lifting his glass of tea. After a sip, he went back to work.

Derrick wasn't sure if he could answer Aaron's question. His mind was nowhere near school. He knew the two people sitting next to him could help him with his struggle, but he also feared opening up to them. Everyone had been praising him for how well he was doing. What would they think if he admitted he was struggling? What impact would that have on their view of his successes? He felt it best to continue as he had been, dealing with this on his own.

The sandwiches came, and Derrick and Breonna spent the meal as people usually spent a meal at Davies Deli, in absolute silence. The sandwiches commanded respect. If a word was spoken before the last bite was eaten, it was as an unspoken rule of all that was delicatessen was broken. At least that's how it felt. Derrick was sure the captivation would wear off after the thirteenth or so sandwich, and he would be able to utter a word or two to someone while eating. But not today.

"Wow," Breonna said after swallowing her final bite. She took a sip of her tea, which an attentive Jasmine quickly refilled.

"Yeah," Derrick responded, which was the appropriate reply. He looked toward the cobbler case and wondered how much room he had left.

Breonna saw him drooling over the dessert. She gave him a backhand to the arm. "Not yet. We'll get there. Be patient."

"I'm just looking," he assured her. Although he knew, hungry or full, he was getting a bowl. Just not yet. He had something to take care of first.

Derrick shifted in his seat to face Breonna, which didn't escape her notice. "Is everything okay?"

"Actually, no," Derrick began. "I need to talk to you about something that's been bothering me. Maybe you can help me with it. I wanted to wait until the timing was right, and now it feels right."

"Okay. Does this have to do with what we talked about earlier?" Breonna asked.

"In a way. That's a separate issue, but it does tie into this."

"Okay. Let's talk about it," Breonna said, shifting in her seat toward him and placing her hands in her lap.

Derrick took a breath and released it. He had prepared for this moment for the last week. Now was the time to tell her. "You remember how I visited your church last week."

"Yeah."

"And you know I have a church that I, in a way, grew up in and have started to attend again."

"Yes. You've mentioned that."

"I was wondering if you'd be willing to come with me to *my* church. I don't want you to feel obligated to just because I visited yours. I want you to come because I'm asking you to. But I also understand that you have your church and family and may feel more comfortable there."

Breonna smiled. "I would love to visit your church, Derrick."

"Really?" Derrick was surprised it was that simple.

"Of course. It's your church. It's about your background, your family history. I said I wanted to get to know all about you. This is part of it."

"Wow. Okay. I didn't think it would be that easy," he admitted with a laugh.

"Stop being silly," she said. "You were willing to visit my church family. You weren't comfortable in the slightest, but you bore through it, and I'm happy and blessed that you tried."

"You could tell I wasn't comfortable?"

Breonna laughed. "Even my dad could tell that. And he could tell it wasn't over intimidation from him. You're a tower compared to him. But my dad understands that God has a place for everyone. I understand the same. Maybe your place is at the church you grew up in? Let God lead you." Breonna pointed at his chest. "Follow His direction and go there, not where I'm at. If you only go to my church because of me and not for God, then, I'm sorry, I don't want you there."

"So, will you go with me this week? I want you to meet some people," Derrick said.

"I'm already there," Breonna said, taking his hand.

Derrick smiled, feeling half a load off his shoulders.

Considering he had only been back once since his three-year absence was the other half load. But he knew that the whole reason he was going back was the burning feeling that he belonged there. He wasn't sure if Breonna would feel that pull, but he wanted her to experience what he did growing up. The love and passion of a small church.

Derrick walked through the parking lot again but didn't see her. He checked his watch, 11:55—service was about to start. He walked the front sidewalk, and one of the ushers came to him, "Everything okay, Derrick?"

"Yeah," Derrick said in a drawn-out sigh. He dialed her number, and six rings later, it went to voice mail. *Well, it isn't off, and she isn't swiping left. Maybe she went to her church after all and left her phone in her car or purse or another building or somewhere....* Derrick returned to the building when he heard the piano cue up.

"If you see a woman, about five-five with shoulder-length dark brown hair," he motioned with his hands at his shoulders, "let her know I'm inside. Third row from the rear on the right."

"Yes, sir," said the usher.

Derrick gave one more pass of the street then headed inside. He figured her dad pulled rank and didn't allow her to come. Either it was him or the small hole-in-the-wall church on the south side of the highway. It didn't bode well for their relationship in either case.

Derrick found his seat, closed his eyes, and took a deep breath. He wanted to focus on the service and not his personal problems. He wanted to feel the way he did the first time he was in the building, but he couldn't. Something kept nagging at him that something wasn't right. He knew that Breonna wasn't the type of person to just push him aside for no reason. She would at least call him to say she couldn't make it.

One song in, and he hadn't heard a word or note. Two, he was more in touch with what was being sung. By song three, he was humming along. Pastor Hayes spoke in front of a swaying choir a verse out of the book of Isaiah. His eyes were closed, trying to remain where he was and not taken back to his life outside when there was a tug on his shirt sleeve. For a moment, he felt relief. He smiled and turned his head, expecting to see one form of an angel. Instead, he saw a short, frightened boy who bore a striking resemblance to her.

"Derrick, you got to come with me now. Something terrible has happened," Ellis said with tears in his eyes. "Come on."

"What? What's wrong?" Derrick said in a loud enough whisper to draw irritated stares.

"Breonna's been in an accident. She's at Mercy Regional, and they're taking her into surgery. You need to come with me now. Let's go."

Derrick's heart sank. He wanted to pass out and nearly did until Ellis took his arm. "Dude, I'm driving. Just leave your car here."

"I walked. I live around the corner," Derrick said.

"Well, okay. Let's go."

Ellis helped the man twice his size to his car, and they drove into Sunday traffic heading to Breonna's side, not knowing what the outcome would be, saying prayers as he hadn't prayed in years, praying as he hadn't since losing another woman he loved.

Chapter
Twenty-Two

"Derrick, it's been ten hours. Go home and get some sleep," Breonna's mother said. Her name was Beverly. Her father was Isaac. Derrick had heard them say something similar at least fifty times since he arrived.

"I'm not going anywhere until I know she's going to be okay," Derrick said as he sat, elbows on his knees, staring into space.

"Then at least go down to the cafeteria and get something to eat," she suggested. "You must be hungry. We'll send Ellis down if we hear anything."

"I'm not hungry. Thank you," he lied, still not making eye contact.

Mrs. Greene sighed and sat next to her husband. Ellis was in another corner, lost in his game—or faking he was lost in a game. He didn't seem to be moving much, just staring at the screen. Derrick felt he was living a rerun. Just about four years ago, he sat in a similar room waiting for doctors to give him the inevitable news. His mom came into the ER with no vitals. With Breonna, he wasn't aware of her status when she came in, and he couldn't bring himself to ask.

Everyone's head shot up when a doctor in green scrubs and a face mask around her neck came through the swinging doors breaking the silence. She walked to the nurse's station, who pointed in their group's direction. Mrs. Greene gripped her husband's arm tightly.

The doctor approached and introduced herself. "I'm the surgeon in charge of your daughter's treatment." The doctor looked over to Derrick, then to Mr. and Mrs. Greene.

"He is fine. He's family," Mr. Greene said.

The doctor gave him a once over then continued. "Your daughter had a serious accident. It didn't look good when she came in, but we were able to stabilize her. She had internal bleeding, and we needed to perform emergency surgery to repair it. We believe we've resolved that issue, but she also experienced serious head trauma, and we won't know the full extent of those injuries until the swelling goes down. Her arm is broken, but that's a minor issue. The major problem we now face is that she's in a coma, and it's anybody's guess when she'll come out of it. Could be hours; could be a couple of days. It depends on how long her body chooses to heal itself. The doctors here will do their best to monitor her condition and give her the best treatment. At this point, the best we can do is to let her rest and wait and see."

"Thank you, doctor," Mr. Green said, shaking her hand. "We appreciate all you have done and for explaining everything to us."

Derrick felt sick. These were the words he remembered from the time his mom was in the hospital—*hard to tell, doing their best*, and *wait and see*—words that plagued him in the background as the doctors talked to his aunt. He was still a minor, so anything serious he heard was hushed whispers.

Then one day, his aunt entered the room and told him they were leaving. They never returned to the hospital. It wasn't until a few days later that she told him his mother had passed. Two weeks later, he turned eighteen. Two weeks after that, she loaded up a U-Haul and moved away from Sunnyvale.

Derrick didn't like hospitals; he hated them. But he wasn't going anywhere until he knew Breonna was going to be okay. This time his age didn't prevent him from knowing her condition. He looked to her parents. They were holding each other. He knew he wasn't family and that he was only there by their good graces. He was thankful for that. Derrick hoped that would continue, because he needed to stay. After all, the woman he loved was here.

Derrick was awakened by the channel changing on the television. The room was empty. Breonna's parents were gone. The only person in the room was a familiar figure sitting in the row across from him.

"Carter?" Derrick asked.

"Who did you expect?"

"Anyone but you," Derreck said.

"I spend quite a bit of time in these halls," Carter explained.

"Is that the reason I couldn't find you on the street?"

"Perhaps," Carter said, staring at the TV.

"I will add the hospital to my list," Derrick said.

Carter remained silent. He flipped the channel. "You can never find good programming on these days. Where's *Gomer Pyle* when you need him?"

"Who?"

Carter took his eyes off the television for the first time

and looked at Derrick, "Well, Golleee," he said in his best impression.

Derrick's eyebrows furrowed, "You lost me, pal."

Carter left the TV on a weather station and tossed the remote on the table. "It doesn't matter. How are you?"

"I've seen better days," Derrick said, adjusting himself, realizing how much he ached. "I guess I've been here all night. Where did Breonna's parents go?"

"I'm not sure. The room was empty when I arrived." Carter sipped on a coffee and set it down. Another was sitting beside it. "The other is for you," he said.

"I don't—" Derrick started, then thought about how much coffee he'd been drinking lately and picked up the cup. "Never mind."

"You have a good heart, Derrick," Carter began. "That's evident with you being here for Breonna."

"But…"

"But what?"

"I don't know. Your comment sound's a bit loaded. Like there's something more that I'm missing."

Carter pouted. "You need to examine your true motives. Are you here for Breonna, or are you here to make up for what you think you lost with your mother? Because you will only hurt Breonna if you're trying to make up for your mom through her."

Derrick sat stunned. Was he trying to do that? He walked to the window overlooking the parking lot. People were driving in and out, going about their business, oblivious to what was going on inside. Lives were hanging in the balance within these walls. Or maybe they did know, and they were running from the choices they had to make.

"I need something to eat," Derrick said. "I'll be in the cafeteria."

He left the waiting room and Carter to the Weather Channel.

Derrick sat sipping on a coffee. He didn't like coffee, but over the last few weeks, he had grown accustomed to it. It made him feel closer to Breonna. He looked over at the pastries. His stomach grumbled, but he couldn't think of eating when she sat comatose in a room above him. His face was locked on a trash bin in his vision range when he felt a hand on his shoulder. He looked up into Isaac Greene's face.

"Have you been here all night?"

Derrick shrugged.

"I appreciate your dedication, son, but you need to go home and get some rest."

"I feel like this is my fault," he said.

"How is this your fault?"

"If I'd never asked her to my church, this never would have happened. I should have left well enough alone. She was happy at your church."

"What makes you say that?"

"She was forever inviting me to go."

"That doesn't mean she was happy."

"Then why did she keep inviting me?"

"Because that's what a Christian does. Reach out to the lost." Mr. Greene sat across from Derrick. "You know, she was searching herself. Why do you think she was so quick to accept your offer to visit your church?"

Derrick didn't know how to answer. He never considered

that Breonna was searching too. He figured she was set in her faith and in her place.

"Not everyone is as set on where the parents are placed. God has a unique opportunity for everyone. She was open to the opportunity that maybe her place was elsewhere. Perhaps even at Faith Community."

"I hadn't considered that. I still feel sorry."

"What for?" Mr. Greene replied. "I raised Beonna to be her own person. If she found a godly man who would lead her and a church that will guide her spiritually, then I support her 100 percent."

"That's the problem, sir. I'm *not* 100 percent. I'm still finding my way. I'm not sure where I am with Christ."

"Oh, I think you do, son. I just think you just need to convince yourself. And you're not far from it. Once you do, there's nothing that will be impossible for you. And that man? I will be proud to know the man that will be the spiritual partner with my Breonna. Don't sell yourself short, Derrick. God has big plans for you." Mr. Greene stood, patted Derrick on the shoulder, and left the cafeteria.

Derrick sat with his now cold coffee between his hands; he had never taken a sip. It was, after all, for Breonna's sake. He did finish his pastry. It was dry but edible. He looked up at the clock and realized it was Monday. He needed to call work, call off, and mention Breonna if her parents hadn't already done so. Today he would miss his scheduled classes and his shift at work. There would be no tearing him away from the hospital.

Derrick considered taking a cup of coffee to Carter to return the favor, but he doubted he would still be in the waiting room, so he went back up empty-handed. When he reached the waiting room, as he expected, Carter was gone.

Another three hours passed. Breonna's parents entered the waiting room as refreshed as distressed parents could be and sat across the room from him. Breonna's parents pleaded with him to go home and get some rest, but Derrick refused.

Derreck's phone buzzed. It was a message from his boss. Mr. Lauder told him to take all the time he needed for him and Breonna. Derrick responded with a quick *thanks* and went back to focusing on the spot on the wall. It hadn't moved—neither had he. For the last few hours he questioned whether God was really there. It was a struggle that began when he lost his mom. And now that it appeared he might lose Breonna, he was close to abandoning any resemblance of faith he had left. How could a loving God allow him to lose both a mom and a potential spouse? It didn't make sense.

He closed his eyes and prayed. It was the second time Derrick had prayed alone. He wasn't sure if his past or current doubts would prevent him from getting through, but for Breonna's sake, it was worth a try.

Chapter
Twenty-Three

Derrick received a call that he was needed back at work. It was the holidays, and they were getting busy and down two employees with both him and Breonna away. Mr. Lauder said he felt for his situation, but he needed him back at the bookstore. Derrick pushed back a little but gave in and agreed to report for his shift that morning.

Derrick spent another night in a waiting room chair. The only difference was that a nurse brought him a pillow and a blanket. He halfway expected to have an angelic alarm clock, but Carter was nowhere to be seen when Derrick woke up the following day. The television channel had been changed to the Weather Channel. That made him curious. He went down to the cafeteria, hoping to run into Breonna's parents so he could let them know he had to leave. He found them at a table with Ellis.

"Good morning, Mr. and Mrs. Greene, Ellis," Derrick said, not entirely sure what he was going to say.

"Good morning, Derrick," Mrs. Greene said. Her father also greeted him. Ellis nodded, then looked back down to his screen. "Did you stay again last night?"

"Yeah," he admitted. "But I have to get going. It appears the bookstore simply can't function with both of us gone." Derrick rolled his eyes, trying to lighten the mood a little. "I need to go home, grab a shower, then head in."

"You may need these," Mr. Greene said, tossing something toward Derrick. It was his car keys. He had forgotten he left his vehicle at the church. "I had Ellis bring your car over last night so you would have your car here."

Derrick snickered at not remembering he didn't have his car, "Thank you. I appreciate that. I had completely forgotten how I got here."

"That's okay, Derrick. It's understandable. Thank you for being here. And for staying with Breonna. You being here made us feel more comfortable leaving," Mrs. Greene said. Mr. Greene nodded.

"I'm glad I could do that for you. I just felt weird leaving."

"When she wakes up, one of us will call you," Mr. Greene said, standing and extending his hand. "Thank you, son."

Derrick accepted his hand. It was the second time Mr. Greene had called him *son*. He realized how good it felt to be addressed as such. Others had used that title with him, but with Mr. Green, he felt a level of respect that hadn't been there for a long time. While he had only known the man for two weeks—and for all he knew, *son* could be a common word in his vocabulary—at that moment, it meant something to him.

"I'll have my phone with me at all times," Derrick said, holding his phone in the air. He turned and headed out the door and headed toward a shift he knew he would not be able to focus on.

After a quick shower and trim, he was out the door. Derrick arrived at work in a fog and didn't even know if he had made it on time or not. He just clocked in and began his day. The world must've been evident on his shoulders to everyone. His coworkers kept their distance, even Brandon, who would normally be sidling up to him for information about the latest in his dating life. It was all business for once. He was glad there was a steady stream of customers. It kept him behind the register most of the night, except for the occasional to run to the back for rolls of register tape.

Simon handled returns and displays. He kept to his business as well. Derrick was almost annoyed. These people knew Breonna. Showing a little bit of concern would be acceptable. It wasn't until near closing that anyone spoke to him directly. It was Mr. Lauder that approached him in the break room and inquired about Breonna. Derrick nearly broke down, explaining the accident and her condition. He apologized again for missing work, to which Mr. Lauder repeated his acceptance of the first apology, and no other was needed. After they parted, his annoyance subsided. He realized he wasn't ready to talk about her just yet.

Derrick looked down at his phone. There were no notifications to reply to, no missed calls. He hoped it was a good sign. A better sign would be a phone call that she was awake and improving. He finished his meal, clocked back in, and finished his shift with no further inquiries about his feelings or Breonna.

Derrick left work as soon as Mr. Lauder turned the key in the lock. He didn't even wait for his regular *good night crew* closing. He just made a beeline to his car and headed out.

But he had to make a stop before driving to the hospital. Aaron would be prepping at Davies Deli, and Derrick had promised to be there on Wednesday. Things had changed, and he wanted to explain in person.

The deli was lit up, and several vehicles were still parked in front of the building. Seeing so many there made him feel better since he wouldn't be able to stay and help. He wasn't so sure about tomorrow or the event itself. He felt divided and wanted to talk to someone who had been there.

Inside were a couple of faces he recognized from college. They were members of a Christian group that was active in the community. He remembered them regularly seeking volunteers to help with various projects. He didn't realize this deli was the one they advertised for Thanksgiving. He had been asked once but didn't accept. *Who has the time or wants to work on their vacation?*

He shook their hands and talked briefly about school and getting past midterms. They directed him to the kitchen area where the smell of stuffing cooking emanated and where Pop and Aaron were. Derrick pushed through the swinging door, and the sound of pots and pans clanging hit him from the left. Another set of students was washing the empties, getting them ready for a new batch. Ahead of him and to the right was Pop and a large mixing bowl. He was dancing to music and stirring in rhythm.

"Derrick, my boy, welcome to where the magic happens," Pop said. "You like Jazz?"

Derrick nodded and had to laugh. "Yes, sir. It's obvious you like it as well?"

Pop did a jig and spun around. "I find it difficult to be creative without it."

"Aaron around?"

"Yes. He's just around the corner there past the ovens."

"Ovens?"

"Yes. We have four now. We got a grant a couple of years ago to help with our Thanksgiving meal. We feed about 150 families now."

"One-hundred fifty? Wow. And all of this came about from your daughter's passing?" Derrick said and quickly regretted saying it. What if he brought up old feelings for the older man?

"Yes! My DeeDee's spirit lives on through what we do here every Thanksgiving. Even my wife's passion exists in this meal," Pop said with a wide grin, holding his stirring spoon up in front of him.

"That's amazing."

"Yes, we even had to expand the kitchen to fit everything," Pop said, spoon pointing toward the ovens, spilling a bit of dressing on the floor.

"Well, Pop. I'll let you get back to your Jazz and dressing. I need to find Aaron."

"Alrighty," Pop said with a jig.

Derrick followed Pop's spoon-wielding directions and soon found Aaron, who himself was prepping for the meal, basting a few turkeys that looked like they had just come out of the oven.

"You're baking them already?" Derrick asked.

"Yes, we used to make them the evening before. But quickly learned that carving became a headache. So, we bake them the day before. Then, right before serving, we carve them. It makes them easier to carve, and it keeps them moister. It worked so well last year that we are doing it again.

"That first year was crazy. We had just the one double oven.

We cooked four turkeys and barely had enough. Last year we had just over 100 families come through here. Pop expects 150 this year. And that's the number of families. When we broke it down, it was close to 600 people."

"That's incredible, Aaron. That's what I need to talk to you about. I don't think I'm going to be able to help out like I said I would."

Aaron set down his baster and looked to Derrick with a cocked head. "Is everything okay?"

"No, it's not. Breonna was in a serious accident. She's over at Mercy right now in a coma. The doctors say she has a broken arm and internal injuries. They did emergency surgery to stop the internal bleeding, but she's still unconscious." Derrick took a breath, realizing he had been rushing his speech.

"Slow down," Aaron said, moving across the table to Derrick, placing his hand on his shoulder. "Just breathe. It's going to be okay."

At first, the statement upset Derrick. How could Aaron know for sure everything was going to be okay? He wasn't a doctor. He wasn't there with her. How could he know? "I—I just don't know Aaron. She has been like this for a couple of days now. I only left the hospital because my job was on the line if I didn't go in. I'm heading back to the hospital now but wanted to talk to you before I did."

"Well, you are free from your obligation here. I won't hold you to it. Family comes first."

"Thank you. I appreciate that," Derrick said. "Can I ask you something else?"

"Sure?"

"What was it like for you, waiting at the hospital, not knowing anything? You said that you and Deborah were not married, but you had access to her. Did Pop help you get access?"

"Well," Aaron grinned. "The hospital was under the impression that I was her fiancé."

"So, you lied to get access to her?"

"Not in so many words. I was with her when she had the episode that landed her in the hospital. At first, the paramedics wouldn't let me ride in the ambulance with her. I was scared because I didn't know what was going on, so I told them I was her fiancé. That got me into the ambulance as well as back into the room with her. Otherwise, I would have been left in the dark."

"I see," Derrick said. He knew that ploy wouldn't work in his case. Her parents knew they had just begun dating, and advancing their relationship that far would cause more issues than it would solve. He was lucky enough to be able to sit in the waiting room.

"I don't know what to do here. I feel lost. I'm scared," Derrick began. He found a stool and sat. He looked to the ground and finally got the nerve to ask the question he came to ask. "Why would God allow this to happen to her? Why would He let a person who follows Him come this close to death? If this is the God you serve, then I'm not sure I want any part of it."

Aaron pulled up another stool and, once seated, stared at the imaginary spot where Derrick seemed to focus. He exhaled. "I don't pretend to have all the answers. I know that's what you came here for. But I don't. That would be doing you a disservice, and it would be misrepresenting God. Some things happen in life we can't explain. Take Deborah, for example. Why did she have to die? I can't answer that. Some could say it was to help save other lives through what we are doing right now with the Thanksgiving ministry. This may have never happened if Deborah was alive today. That may sound cruel, but it is the only way I know how to explain it.

"We each have a God orchestrated plan for our life, Derrick. And those events can lead non-believers to seek God in a way that wouldn't have happened through another individual. Meaning, there are people in this world only *you* can reach. Be it through your life experience, education, or future, all of those events can minister to people.

"I choose to see Deborah's passing as a doorway to minister to others, and as Pop says, this Thanksgiving ministry is part of that."

"So, what is Breonna's accident supposed to mean?"

"Only God knows the answer to that right now. Time will tell the reasoning for it. It could be a wake-up call for her Christian walk. It could be a way to reach others for Him through her testimony from this accident. There are many things it could be."

Derrick knew it couldn't be a message for her. He saw no way that could be a reason. She led a good Christian life. But he found it odd that God would use pain and suffering of one individual to bring others to Him.

"Why would God allow her to be in pain over someone else. That's just cruel. Where is the justification in that?"

"It happened all the time in the Bible," Aaron answered. "Take Paul. He was in prison. He was beaten, shipwrecked, stoned—all for the cause of Christ. He allowed those instances to draw others to God. He did it gladly. If his pain meant another soul would be won, he was all for it. And if Breonna is a true follower of Christ, then her accident would be a small price to pay if it draws people to Christ."

Derrick chewed on that comment. Could Breonna's accident be a message to him? Right now, all it did was make him angry. Why would God use one accident to take his mother's life, and another accident to reach him? That made no sense. But there was some truth to what Aaron said. He knew that if it meant saving someone, Breonna would have accepted the mission. She would want to be right where she is.

But is she lying in that bed for me? Is she at death's door to help save my soul?

Chapter
Twenty-Four

Derrick, you need to get here quick," said an alarmed voice on the phone.

Derrick expected the worse, that Breonna was taking her final breath, and he needed to say his goodbyes. But the voice was not in tears. It was elated.

"What is it, Ellis? What's wrong?" Derrick asked, in case he misread his inflection.

"Breonna is awake. She's awake, Derrick!" Ellis almost screamed into the phone. "You need to get over here now!"

"I'm on my way," Derrick said and ended the call. He jumped out of bed. It was still dark. He didn't know what time it was. He wasn't even sure what day it was. But he dressed as quickly as possible, pulling his hoodie over his head. His eyes landed on the illuminated face of his alarm clock. 4:37 AM. No wonder hew felt dizzy and confused. He had fallen asleep a mere three hours ago.

Despite the mental haze, he grabbed his keys and headed for the door. The crisp air hit his nose and lungs like a shot of adrenaline. He took a couple of deep breaths and soon was wide awake. But his car was a different matter. When the weather was this cold, he had to wait for his old friend to warm up. It was the longest five minutes of his life. Once the temperature gauge made the slightest movement, he dropped the transmission into drive, said a quick prayer, and was on his way to the hospital.

His car hit a dip in the road, and his head thumped against the roof. He looked down and realized he was going way too fast. His first thought was the officer behind the mirrored glasses and his stern warning. Derrick eased off the gas and hoped the guy didn't patrol this end of town. His prayer must've worked because every light he approached turned green for him, like a carpet being laid for royalty. He was parading down relatively empty roads. The traffic was still another couple of hours away.

After being at the hospital a few times the last couple of days, he easily found a spot. He didn't want to be hot and sweaty when he saw Breonna or her parents, so he took his time and panic-rushed as slowly as he could into the building and up to the third floor. There was no one in the waiting room where he had spent a couple of nights, but the blanket and pillow were still on the chair in the corner.

Derrick backtracked to the nurses station. "Excuse me, Nurse? Can you tell me where the Greene family is? I received a call to meet them in the waiting room," Derrick said, figuring half-truths were okay in this instance. Ellis was part of the family.

"I'm not sure, sir," the nurse said, checking her charts. "I just came on shift twenty minutes ago. The waiting area was empty when I got here. I'm sorry. Who is the patient?"

"Breonna Greene. She was a car accident victim. She was

in a coma, but I received a call from the family that she had awakened. They asked me to come in," Derrick said. "Can you find a family member for me?"

The nurse nodded. "Please have a seat, sir. I will see if I can reach the family."

Derrick opened his mouth to say more but thought the better of it. "Thank you. I'll be in the waiting area," he said.

Derrick went back into the waiting room and found another person sitting in a chair near the TV watching the Weather Channel.

"Another front is moving in," the man said. "Hope Pop is prepared for the possibility of rain."

Derrick let out a chuckle. "Pop is prepared for anything, Carter. You should know that by now."

"Hmmm," he said. "He is a wise man. Definitely has spunk."

Derrick laughed out loud this time. "That he does." Derrick looked back at the nurse's station. She had yet to move from her desk. He hoped she was letting her fingers do the walking and was notifying the Greenes that he was here.

"Carter, what are you doing here?"

"I get around from time to time when I am needed," he said, looking up to Derrick, then turning his attention back to the forecast.

Aaron's words and his own questions flooded Derrick's mind. "I need to ask you something."

"Ask away. I'm good at answering questions."

"Why is Breonna going through this? Why did God cause this to happen to her? Was her accident a way of getting to me?" Derrick didn't wait for a reply but continued. "This isn't her fault. I'm the one who strayed from God. Why am I not the one in there? It's the way you worked with Deborah. She was the one who strayed. She is the one who got sick. Why aren't I the one in there?"

"Derrick, everything *does* happen for a reason. And I will tell you the same thing I told Aaron—I don't know why or how. I'm given my assignment, and I do my best to lead people back to the Lord."

"Aaron said that since Breonna's faith is strong enough to get through this, it could be the reason why it happened to her. Her body will heal, and her faith will not fail her. But if the situation were reversed, maybe my faith wouldn't be so strong."

"Aaron is a wise man. He has been through a lot. You should listen to his counsel."

"But if this were happening to her for my sake, shouldn't God know that I lost my mom to a car accident and that another car accident could drive me from him?"

Carter turned to Derrick and looked into his eyes. "Has it?"

Derrick thought about the past couple of weeks, being around Aaron, his couple of times back at church, and him just talking to God again. He considered how strong Breonna's faith was, and how it had been an example to him. He had his answer. "No, not in the slightest. The truth is, I've been in prayer more now than I ever have."

"So, you think Breonna would say this accident, while it may take a while for her to heal, should be accepted with open arms, knowing that her pain has strengthened your relationship with the Lord?"

Derrick folded his arms and rubbed his beard in thought. He knew the answer. "She would've gotten into that car knowing what was going to happen. That's the type of person she is. She's sacrificial. It's beyond what I deserve."

"Ahhh, but Derrick, my friend," Carter said, tipping his cap back with a smile. "That's not *your* choice to make. Breonna will fall in love with who she falls in love with. The Lord will lead her to the man she's meant to be with."

"And you think that's me?"

"Perhaps it is, perhaps it's not. I can't mess around in matters of the heart," Carter said with a sly smile. "The boss tends to get upset when I do that."

"Who, God?"

"No, smaller. Blonde hair, blue eyes—never mind," Carter said with a chuckle. "The point is, you make your life what it is and let her decide whom she's going to love, and you are free to love her back. It doesn't matter who you are or who you've been. If she loves you, take it for what it's worth. And go with it."

Derrick knew Carter was right. He had been hiding behind who he thought Breonna should be with for too long and never considered who Breonna wanted to be with. And for the past few months, that person was him. Everyone knew it but him, rather everyone accepted it but him. He had been trying the past couple of weeks, letting his defenses down, but it was still difficult to talk about. But why should he keep his feelings hidden behind his fears? He loved her. It was time for everyone to know it.

There was a swishing of doors behind them. Carter looked over his shoulder, then back to Derrick with a grin. "There's your ride."

Derrick turned to see a nurse. She went to her companion at the desk and was pointed toward him. The desk nurse looked at him, thanked the other nurse, and headed in his direction.

"Mr. Anders?"

"Yes, I'm Derrick Anders," Derrick said.

"Will you please come with me? The family is asking for you."

Derrick stood and shared goodbyes with Carter.

"Thank you for everything, Carter. I can see what my mom saw in you. God bless you."

As Derrick turned to leave, he could've sworn he saw tears in the old angel's eyes. "Thank you, Derrick. That means a lot coming from you."

"Right this way, sir," the nurse said, leading Derrick back to another angel in his life and quite possibly his future.

Chapter
Twenty-Five

Derrick followed the nurse around two corners, passing rooms with hums, beeps, and television noises until they came to a room that was eerily silent. He could hear faint conversation through the partially open door. The nurse knocked, announcing they were entering. Derrick prepared for the worst. He never saw his mom after her accident, but from what his aunt said, it was probably best that he hadn't. She never went into detail, and he never asked.

"Mr. and Mrs. Greene. I have Mr. Anders with me. May we come in?"

"Yes. Please come in," answered a familiar voice, making Derrick smile. He could hear her parents telling her to take it easy. *Not likely*, he thought to himself. *That's not Breonna's style.*

The nurse opened the door for Derrick and stood back. "If you need anything, give us a buzz," she said with a smile.

"Thank you, nurse," Derrick said, stepping into the room. The dividing curtain was drawn partway. He had to step around it; it was like he was being announced on a talk show. As he made his way around, his heart was trying to escape his chest. He took a breath to calm himself. Once into the room, he first saw her parents. Breonna's mom was in a chair beside the bed, and her father was standing behind her. Ellis was on the other side of the bed, video game still in his hands.

Then Derrick saw Breonna.

She remained the most beautiful creature he had ever seen. The cast on her left arm went from her wrist to her shoulder. That same side of her face was blackened and bruised. Her eye was closed and puffy, and her jaw bore the same signs of wear. But through it all, her patented smile was fighting to shine through. He saw it, and it was all he could do to fight his tears back.

"Hey," she said.

"Hey," he said back.

The room went back to silence. Derrick felt he was on the spot being the newcomer. He wasn't sure what else to say. "Sorry I'm late. The traffic was a nightmare." He grinned. Maybe the comment was ill-timed or inappropriate because everyone remained quiet. Until Breonna started to giggle, then her parents laughed. Ellis remained enthralled with his game.

"How are you feeling?" Derrick asked, unsure where else to go, even though she probably answered the question a dozen times now.

"I'm still trying to figure that out," Breonna said. "I'm a bit uncomfortable and in some pain. But I may have this machine over here to thank for that," Breonna said with a slight nod toward the drip machine she was hooked up to.

"I'm glad you're back. We've been praying for you," Derrick said, nodding over to her parents.

"I heard you're going to have to pay rent out there soon."

"I haven't been here that long," Derrick lied.

"Oh please, your pillow and blanket are still out there, Der," Ellis said, finally taking his attention off his game. "Breonna, he has a bed out there. He wouldn't leave. He's worse than that old man."

Derrick looked at Ellis. "Which old man?"

"You know, the guy in the matching brown coat and hat," Ellis said, tipping an imaginary hat. "I've seen him in the waiting area, the cafeteria, and walking in the hall back here. He must have someone he's visiting."

Derrick knew Ellis was referring to Carter. "Yes, I think he has family on this floor too." He didn't know what else to say. He didn't need additional questions should they be seen together.

"Oh, my," Breonna said with a startle.

Breonna's mom turned to her. "What's wrong, sweetie?"

"Nothing. Just what Ellis said brought back a memory. Strangest thing. Must be the medication."

"What did you remember?" her father asked.

"Remember the rummage sale over at the Catholic church, Mom?"

"Yeah," her mom said, not quite sure where the conversation was going.

"Well," she began, then stopped and turned to Derrick. "You'll remember this, I told you about when I found your mom's headbands. The vendor who sold them to me was very kind. He said they were specially made for me. That man wore a brown tweed coat and matching hat. When Ellis said that, it brought back the memory of buying those headbands and my purse."

"Say that again?" Derrick said, not believing what he had just heard.

"The vendor at the rummage sale wore a matching coat and hat. Why, is something wrong?"

Derrick didn't know how to respond. He knew it had to have been Carter, but why? Why would Breonna getting his mom's headbands matter so much, other than opening the door to conversation?. As Derrick recalled, he hadn't spoken to Breonna before he saw his mom's headband on her head. Did Carter have something to do with her finding those headbands? Did he guide her to them to open the door to them talking?

"No, nothing is wrong. It's just interesting that you mention that the man in the lobby looks like the man you remember at the rummage sale."

"Oh, well, he was nice, and I received a memory of your mother," Breonna said, touching her head with her good arm. She was wearing one of them, keeping her messy hair out of her face. "They certainly are beautiful, Derrick."

Derrick wanted to say that they looked good on her but wasn't sure what type of reaction it would get from her parents. "Thank you. My mom made them special. Glad that someone special was able to get them." He didn't look up from Breonna's stare to see her parent's reaction.

Breonna yawned and smiled at her parents. Their instincts kicked in, and her mom said, "Well, honey, we should let you get some rest." She tenderly touched Breonna's good leg.

"Sleep?" Breonna said. "I've been sleeping for three days, according to you and the doctors."

As if on cue, the nurse came back in and said that they needed to take Breonna back for a CT scan, now that she was awake.

"We'll be downstairs eating some breakfast."

Well, be back up in—a couple of hours?" Breonna asked the nurse.

"That should be fine. Just ask at the front desk. Someone will usher you back when she's back in her room," the nurse said.

"May I have a minute with Derrick, please?" Breonna asked.

Her parents looked at each other, then to the nurse, who looked to her watch. She grimaced. "Five minutes. I need to roll a patient anyhow. I'll be right back."

Breonna's family left the room escorted by the nurse, leaving the two of them alone.

"Hey," Derrick said, sitting in the chair her had vacated.

"Oh, no, you don't. Don't start that again," Breonna said, laughing, then grimacing in pain.

"Don't do that to yourself, Bree. What is it? Broken ribs?"

"No, just bruised. They thought they were, but now that the swelling has gone down, they say they're only bruised. But the meds must be wearing off because I'm starting to feel every one of them."

Derrick started to tear up again. He didn't want to cry in front of her. He was supposed to be the strong one and spur her on to recovery.

"Hey," she said.

Derrick looked up and met her eyes.

"I'm going to be okay. The doctor said they stopped the internal bleeding, and I should make a full recovery. I may lose some rotation in my arm because of where the fracture is, but other than that, they say I'm fine. God had his hand on me."

Derrick nodded. "I know." He didn't want to mention his talk with Aaron and their belief that her accident was a means to draw him closer to the Lord.

"So, have you really been sleeping on a chair in the waiting room?"

Derrick half laughed. "Yeah, I've been here. I did leave for a bit. Mr. Lauder made it clear that I was needed at work. He sends his prayers, by the way. And everyone else sends their well wishes… in their own way."

"I'm glad you finally went home to get some rest. I can't believe you slept in a chair and waited here for me," Breonna said, her good hand reaching for his. He accepted it.

"I didn't know where else to be," Derrick said. "I just kept praying that you'd be okay, that God would heal you. I'm glad He still answers prayers."

"I'm glad to hear you're praying," Breonna said, squeezing his hand.

"Yeah, well, you would be amazed at how much praying I've done lately. And it doesn't all revolve around your healing."

"Really? Care to share?"

Derrick looked to the ground. "Someday," he said softly.

His thoughts swam back to Carter, and he was nervous about how to ask, or even bring it up, but since Ellis had already opened the door, he used that route. "So, you said the guy who sold you the headbands was wearing a dark tweed coat and hat?" He looked up to see her reaction.

"Yes. He kinda looked out of place. It was warm out, and he was wearing that coat and hat. All the vendors were older ladies or teens selling stuff to raise money for a mission trip. He just stood out; probably why I remember him so well. Anyway, yes. I passed by with my aunt, and he commented about the band I was wearing. Then he pointed out the tray of the ones your mom made. I also bought a purse from him."

"A purse? What did it look like?" Derrick asked out of curiosity.

"Tan shoulder strap purse. He gave me a good deal on it, the outer zipper—"

"was stuck." Both of them said at the same time.

Derrick laughed. "I think you got my mom's purse too. She had one just like it, with a stuck zipper."

"Well, it's unstuck now," Breonna giggled, then grimaced. "I don't know how, but the accident did it. When my mom handed me my purse to get my headband out of it, I noticed that the zipper had busted open."

Derrick was curious. His mom had loved that purse. Even though it had the near welded zipper, she would carry that purse everywhere. Not that a zipper made or broke a purse's function, it just seemed to him that his mom would want a good purse.

"Can I see it?" he asked, unsure of whether he was breaking some female code.

"Sure. It's on the arm of that chair." Breonna pointed to the chair behind him.

He smiled as he picked it up. The minute he saw it, he could see his mother searching around the living room, looking for it so she could head off to work. He remembered thinking if she had a normal purse, like other moms, she would never lose it—but she always seemed to misplace the shoulder strap purse.

"Was there anything in the pouch when the zipper seam broke?"

Breonna gave a curious face. "It didn't occur to me to look."

"May I?"

Breonna shrugged her good shoulder, "Go ahead. I'm just as curious as you are."

Derrick reached into the small pocket of the purse, fully

expecting to pull out nothing but pocket lint or maybe a twelve-year-old stick of Wrigley's. But his fingers found something quite different. It was cold and round. His face must've revealed something, because Breonna's face changed expression as well.

"What?" she asked.

Derrick pulled out a key. "Is this yours?" he asked.

"No, I've never seen it before," Breonna said. "It must've belonged to your mom."

"I don't know. I've never seen her with a key like this. Heck, I've never even *seen* a key like this before," Derrick said, holding the odd-shaped key to his eyes. It was round with a circle at one end and two teeth on the other. "It almost looks like a skeleton key."

"I wonder what it goes to?" Breonna asked, sitting up in pain but with the curiosity of a detective on a major case.

"I don't know, but I'm going to find out," Derrick said. "And I know exactly who to ask about it."

Chapter
Twenty-Six

Derrick kissed Breonna on the unbruised side of her forehead and headed back to the waiting area. Only Breonna's family sat there. Carter was gone.

"Did you see an older gentleman sitting in here when you came out?"

"You mean the man in the coat and hat?" Ellis asked, raising his eyebrows.

Derrick was found out. He had little way of hiding it. Both parents looked stunned at him, at the thought that this person could be real and not a figment of a child's imagination.

"Yes," Derrick said with a rush in his voice, "Which way did he go?"

"There was no one out here when we got here, sweetie," Beverly Greene said.

"Okay. Ummm," Derrick was not sure what to do. He wanted to stay for Breonna, but he needed answers about the key, and he was sure Carter held those answers. "I'll be right back. I won't be long."

Derrick turned and went to the nurse's station, but they

were no help. They hadn't seen him leave either. He exhaled deeply and headed for the elevator. Two floors down and to the right, a dozen or so people were in the cafeteria, but no one with a tweed coat or floppy brimmed cap. He asked the cashier, but he hadn't seen anyone matching Carter's description either. Derrick headed down into the main lobby, but saw no one that even remotely resembled Carter.

"Where could he be?" Derrick muttered. "Just when I need him, too."

Derrick returned to the waiting room and sat across from the Greenes, apologizing for running out so fast.

"So, who is the man in the coat and hat?" Ellis said, putting his game away.

Derrick didn't know where to begin or what to say about Carter Jennings. The truth was definitely not on the table. Now that all six eyes were on him, he realized he needed to offer some plausible explanation so they wouln't think Carter harbored some ill will toward their daughter.

"He's just a friend. Well, not so much a friend that you call up and hang out with; more of a—" then it hit him, part of the truth couldn't hurt.

"Actually, he knew my mother. I guess he volunteers at the church where Breonna bought her hairbands. I haven't spoken to him since my mom passed, but we recently got back in touch. He has a friend in the hospital here who isn't doing well, and he was here visiting." Part of the truth. He was a friend, which made Breonna a friend, so he wasn't *really* lying.

"We were talking out here before the nurse called me back. When Breonna mentioned the connection, I wanted to ask him more about some of the things the church may have had. My aunt sold many of my mom's things. I thought he might have more answers for me. That's all."

Derrick hated to lie to them. Even stretching the truth made him feel uncomfortable, but what was he supposed to say? An angel of God was following him around, sending him messages, and he may have just gotten the biggest one of all? They would put him in a strightjacket until they could cart him away to the psychiatric ward.

They seemed convinced. He hoped there would be no follow-up questions and that they would just leave it at that. So far, so good. He stood up, said his goodbyes, and headed for the only place he knew that Carter might be.

The sun was well up and doing its business of heating the morning. He was careful to check the lobbies and cafeterias on his way out, just in case, but there were no signs of Carter anywhere. He hoped he was on a bus or in a cab on his way back to the central library. It had only been an hour, so he was sure he'd beat the city bus there. Once the defroster did its job, he was out of the lot and on his way.

Two hours later, there was still no sign of Carter. Derrick made it to the library, but they hadn't seen him inside, and he didn't believe Carter would loaf around outside, but he looked anyhow. No luck. He watched the nearest bus stop for a half-hour, then gave up. He needed to get back to Breonna.

Derrick held the key in his hand, knowing he was missing something. How long had that key been in that pouch? For all he knew, that zipper was stuck when his mom bought the thing, and the key belonged to its previous owner, especially if she purchased it used. It looked like a key you would see in the movies that would open the door to a secret passage. He thought of every door in the house, but there were no locked doors nor old-fashioned elements of any kind. This key was unique, and it had a specific purpose. He closed his fist around it and prayed.

"I don't know if this is some kind of coincidence or a message from you, Lord, but please help me find what this key goes to and why my mother needed it."

Derrick opened his eyes. He knew there was not much else he could do. Another bus pulled up—no tweed in sight. He put his car in gear and drove back to the hospital.

Derrick sat across from Breonna in a chair, twiddling the key in his hands. She sat up, finishing the Jell-O that came with her lunch. Her parents were satisfied with the doctor's review of her case that she was out of the woods and only needed monitoring for another forty-eight hours. She apologized that Breonna would still be admitted through the holiday but explained that it would be better to be safe than sorry. They agreed and felt safe enough to leave Breonna in Derrick's care while they left for lunch. Derrick was relieved because it would give them time to talk.

"I'm sorry you couldn't find your friend," Breonna said.

"It's okay. He seems to find me when he needs to. I know this key means something. When the timing is right, he'll come around again," Derrick said, his eyes still locked on the key.

"It's funny how all this seems tied together, that your friend—Carter is his name?"

"Yes, Carter."

"It's funny how all of this seems to include him. The hairbands, the purse, you seeing him at work and here. If I were paranoid, I would say he's stalking us."

Derrick laughed, lowering the key and looking to Breonna. He wanted to tell her, but how would that help? Even he didn't fully understand it. He certainly didn't want to tell her she was lying in a hospital bed because God wanted to win his soul. What sense would that make? If she did believe it, would she hate him for his lack of belief? Derrick shook his head.

"What?" Breonna asked, her good eye probing him.

"Carter isn't stalking anyone. He's just someone who likes to help people. He's much like you. You wanted me to discover who I was and to get closer to God, right?"

"Yes. And this Carter did something to help you get closer to God?"

Derrick was quiet a moment in contemplation. Then he nodded, "I guess you can say that if I hadn't met him, I would still be questioning."

"And now you're not?"

Derrick looked to the window. The blackout blinds were partially open, revealing a brilliant blue sky. Derrick smiled. "I don't think so. Both he and you have brought me into a realization of who God is. All of these little reminders I keep finding have been part of a bigger plan to draw me back to Him."

"Little reminders?"

Derrick sighed, a bit nervous because he was treading on the truth. "The headbands, a book I found at the bookstore, my mom's Bible, this key," he said, holding up the key toward her. "God has placed them all to draw me back to Him."

Derrick sat in silence. Breonna matched his demeanor. He went back to focusing on the sky outside. "I've just been through a lot the last couple of weeks. Then this happened to you. And I started to feel like it was a challenge to all the progress I have made. But I realized something, and it was Carter that helped me realize it."

Derrick paused, hoping she would ask, because he couldn't say the next part without her guidance.

"What did Carter help you realize?"

"About what's happened to you. It didn't shake my faith. In fact, it drew me closer to God." Derrick took a breath. "I guess I blamed Him for taking my mom. I hadn't realized it until recently. I had shut God out of my life. I stopped going to church, stopped reading, stopped praying. I still believed in God, but faith was always for someone else. I had no time for it. I guess I felt that He gave up on me, so why should I take the time for Him?

"So, when this happened to you, I should've resorted to that feeling again. But I didn't." Derrick sighed. "I have been searching for answers for the last couple of weeks and praying for Him to show me true faith. And—" Derrick took another breath. "And when this happened to you, I found that faith."

Derrick looked back from staring at the sky and gazed on Breonna. She was in tears. Derrick realized he had said too much. He was ready for her to either tell him to leave or teach him what true faith was about.

Breonna caught her breath. Derrick saw a couple of washcloths on the counter. He handed her one, and she wiped her tears.

"I've been praying for you, Derrick," Breonna began. She took another deep breath and released it. "I know you've been struggling, and I didn't want to force you into making a decision. I've enjoyed spending time with you over the past couple of weeks. It's only made me pray harder for God to touch you and to change your heart toward Him."

"Well, He did," Derrick said. He reached out and took her hand.

Breonna started to laugh through her tears. "I just didn't think He would answer my prayer so boldly. Why couldn't He just send you an angel to set you right?"

Derrick laughed, then squeezed her hand. "You're my angel. I love you, Breonna."

Breonna's eyes filled with tears again, leaving her speechless. Derrick was hoping for a quick reply, the delay was killing him. She took a deep breath and released it.

"I love you too, Derrick."

There was a knock on the door and a raised-octave motherly voice. "Sweetie, it's Mom. You awake?"

Breonna quickly wiped her eyes with her good hand and hid the cloth. Derrick sat back in the chair. Mrs. Greene came around the curtain, alone. She smiled, walked up to Breonna, and ruffled her hair. "How are you feeling?"

"Better. I just want to get out of here," Breonna said, shifting in the bed.

"Soon, dear. It won't be long."

"Guess you won't be reshelving books anytime soon," Derrick said with a chuckle.

"Are you making fun of my cast?" Breonna laughed.

"Who me? Naww. I wouldn't do such a thing."

"So, Derrick, what are your plans for Thanksgiving?" Mrs. Greene asked.

Mrs. Greene's offer reminded him that even though Aaron told him to take the time to be with Breonna, he was originally supposed to be at Davies Deli.

"I was going to be helping at Davies Deli with their community Thanksgiving event. But things have changed."

"What things?" Breonna asked.

"Well, I need to be here with you."

"What for? I'm fine," Breonna said a bit more firmly than he'd like to hear.

Derrick looked to Mrs. Greene.

"Don't look at me. You're on your own. If we can't control her, I wish you all the luck with that."

Breonna was still staring at him with raised eyebrows. She looked up at the clock. It showed 10:50. "What time were you supposed to meet Aaron?"

"Two," Derrick said.

"Derrick!" Breonna scolded.

Derrick looked to the ground again. He felt like a dog that had been scolded for soiling the carpet.

"I want you to get up and head over to the Deli and fulfill your promise to Aaron."

Derrick held out a finger, about to protest, "But—"

"I wouldn't do it, son," a deep voice resonated. Mr. Greene had appeared out of nowhere from around the curtain. "I gave up challenging the Greene women a long time ago. You best learn now if you want a long healthy life. If you're expected somewhere, go on."

"What I want you to do is kiss me on the forehead and get over to Aaron and do what you promised you'd do. And that goes for tomorrow as well. You need to be there if he's feeding the community. I'm a big girl. I'll be fine. And I will be here when you're done."

Derrick nodded and stood. "I'll give Aaron your best," Derrick said. He kissed Breonna on the forehead, said his goodbyes to her parents, and dialed Aaron to tell him he was on his way.

Chapter
Twenty-Seven

Derrick pulled up to Davies Deli, and the "Closed: Preparing for Thanksgiving Day Meal" sign was prominent in the window. The parking lot was as full as it was the previous day. Heads were bopping about through the windows, and Derrick made his way into the building as quickly as he could. He was feeling a new passion for getting things going.

Aaron met him at the door. "Glad you could make it. Good to hear Breonna's recovery update."

"I'm sorry I'm late," Derrick said. "My plan was not to be here at all, but a certain stubborn inpatient lectured me on the finer points of keeping my word."

Aaron laughed. "I know the type. I may not have known Deborah very long, but I learned quickly that she was strong-willed. I'm confident our life together would've been filled with moments of her putting me in my place regarding my priorities."

Derrick laughed. "Slow down, we're not that far yet. We just barely admitted our love for each other. I don't think nuptials is going to happen next week."

"Fair enough. Just don't let life pass you by waiting for the right moment, because it'll never come. You have to dive in together and work at it together, and you will succeed together. But, okay, enough of the brotherly advice. We have work to do," Aaron said, leading him through the swinging door into the kitchen.

"We have the turkey and dressing ready. They've cooled and are ready to carve. Have you ever carved a turkey before?" Aaron led him into the area where he had seen him prepping and cooking the birds on Tuesday night. The tables were covered with turkeys, and a couple of people were working on them already.

"Being the man of the family, that's one thing I can do fairly well. Mom let me start when I was sixteen. I carved our Thanksgiving turkey for two years before she passed. I've carved my own ever since."

"That's good to know," Aaron said, handing him the handle of a carving knife. Derrick took it. "That blade is insanely sharp, so be careful. Don't lose any digits on my watch."

"Gotcha," Derrick answered and went to work on the first bird in front of him. It took him a second to get the feel of the knife and cutting a cold bird instead of a piping hot one.

"Don't let anything go to waste. When we serve, perfect slices don't matter. We're not about presentation. Getting people fed is what's important. So, get all the meat on top and underneath, even the scraps. They're all used."

Derrick considered the bird in front of him. "How big is this thing anyhow?"

"Most of these turkeys are thirty pounds plus," Aaron said. "We get a good deal from a local farm that raises them. They raise, butcher, and package them expressly for our event. The company reached out to Pop two years ago after they read about us in the paper."

Derrick laughed.

"What's so funny?"

"An article in the paper," Derrick said, rotating his bird to start cutting the other side. "Aren't *you* the writer of the paper?"

"Not that piece, no." Aaron laughed. "It wasn't the publication I write for. But I have written articles supporting Pop."

"Ah, okay then. So, Pop gets deals on everything for this meal?"

"Just about. We get donations from our suppliers—just like you picked up those extra napkins. It may not seem like much, but napkins can get expensive. So that little donation saved us from having to use the ones we buy for normal business."

"Interesting," Derrick said. "All of this for one lunch you provided the community?"

"Amazing, right? Deborah would be proud," Aaron said.

For the next couple of hours, Derrick, Aaron and their crew carved every turkey, leaving little on the bone. Aaron showed him how to find those little places where turkey meat liked to hide; the joints and underbelly were all trimmed. They filled the steam pans up, and before Derrick knew it, they had enough sliced turkey to feed an army. They wrapped the pans and placed them in a rack and back into the cooler.

Nothing but carcasses lined the tables now. If Derrick didn't know what was going on, it would have given him the heebie-jeebies. "So, how much turkey is here?"

Aaron looked up to the ceiling and did a quick calculation. "Thirty-pound turkeys, twelve turkeys, what is that—360 pounds? About a quarter pound per person That'll feed just over 1,400."

"We'll see that many people here tomorrow?"

"Who knows? Better to have extra than not enough. Whatever is leftover we send to a local shelter. Not everyone can or will make the trek here."

Aaron looked to the helpers. "You two can clean things up?"

"Yes, sir," the football player-looking one said. "We have it under control."

"Great. If you need us, we'll be up front. I need to go over a few details with my friend here," Aaron said, pointing to Derrick.

Aaron led them to their spot at the counter. "Coffee?" he asked.

Derrick nodded with a cringed grin.

"What's wrong? You don't like coffee?"

Derrick shook his head.

"I've seen you drink it. Now don't go saying you were doing it to be nice."

Derrick nodded. "Sorry. I've never cared for it much."

"What about cocoa, then? We have a machine."

"That sounds great. I can go for a cup of cocoa."

"Marshmallows?" Aaron laughed.

"How else do you drink cocoa?"

"Coming right up." Aaron disappeared.

Derrick leaned upon the counter. He pulled out his key, and his eyes again locked on it. Maybe if he stared it down, it would reveal its secret.

Aaron returned with four cups of cocoa, mounded with marshmallows. He set two across the counter for their carving partners and gave one to Derrick.

"What's that? It looks like a skeleton key."

"It sure does hold secrets in its closet," Derrick said, setting the key on the counter and picking up this cup.

Aaron came around the counter and sat. He picked up the key, raised it to eye level, and stared it down as Derrick had done. "I'm not sure I've seen a key like this outside of movies. It looks like it hides a mysterious treasure. Where did you get it?"

"I found it in my mom's purse. Remember, Breonna bought a couple of my mom's hairbands from a rummage sale? Well, I just found out that she also found a purse. The purse had an outside pocket with a stuck zipper. That is until after Breonna's accident. The accident somehow broke the zipper. When I was with her yesterday, I looked in the pocket, and that key was there. It very well could've belonged to my mom."

"Interesting," Aaron said, setting the key down in front of Derrick.

"I have no clue what it goes to." Derrick took another sip and picked up the key, twiddling it in his hand. "My mom had nothing that I can think of that would fit a key like that."

The two students who had been helping them came into the dining area. "All cleaned up, Aaron. What's next?" asked the football player.

"See if they need any help with the stuffing. We're packing it the same way, in the liners. Oh, and I made you some hot cocoa."

"Gotcha," said the football player.

"Nice key," said the other student. He pushed up his glasses, "You don't want to lose that. They don't make copies as easy as you think they would. My uncle learned the hard way."

"Copies?" Derrick said. "You know what this key belongs to?"

"Sure. It's a safety deposit box key. It's old, but they still make 'em."

"How can you be sure?" Aaron asked.

"My mom works in a bank. I've seen more than my share of safety deposit box keys before."

Derrick looked to Aaron, then back to the genius. "What bank would that be?"

"First Bank of Houston. She's a manager there."

"That's where my mom did her banking. I'm having difficulties with the same place regarding her accounts," Derrick said.

"People store all kinds of thing in safety deposit boxes—banking documents, wills, photographs, even collectibles. I have one. It's where I keep my sports cards and comic books I don't want damaged."

An excitement built in Derrick. Could his mom have a safety deposit box? If she did, what would she put into it? Derrick shook his head.

"What's wrong, Derrick?" Aaron asked.

"What if all this time, the mortgage paperwork I've been digging for is in that box?" Derrick looked at his watch.

"It's too late to go today," Aaron said after checking his. "Yeesh, and tomorrow is a holiday."

"Dang-it," Derrick said, deflated.

"Well, if it's there today, it'll be there on Friday morning. You can go then."

"Dang-it," Derrick repeated.

"What now?"

"It's the day after Thanksgiving. I go to work at 8 AM. The bank doesn't open till 9:00."

"Go after you get off, Derrick," the boy said. "It's a Friday. They'll be open late, till 6:00, I believe."

Derrick took a big breath and released it. "Don't really have a choice, do I? It'll have to wait. Thanks for your help. I'm glad someone knew their stuff."

The boy acknowledged Derrick, and he and the jock returned to the kitchen with their cocoa.

Derrick studied the key again. "There's something else interesting about this key."

"Let me guess," Aaron said knowingly, "the vendor at the rummage sale is familiar to the both of us."

"How did you know?" Derrick asked, lowering the key and meeting Aaron's eyes.

"I once found a Bible in much the same way as Breonna found those hairbands and the purse," Aaron admitted. "I can only assume who was behind such a discovery."

"I'm still in awe over Carter. He visited me in the hospital waiting room while I was waiting to see Breonna."

Aaron started to laugh. "Let me guess; Weather Channel?"

"Yes. He said that there's nothing else good on."

"Yeah, that's where I first met Carter. I didn't know who he was until later. Deborah's the one who told me he was an angel. I didn't fully believe her until he appeared to me later, after she had passed."

Derrick felt a sudden relief. It almost made him feel guilty. Deborah had passed away, but Breonna is going to live. "I'm sorry, Aaron. About Deborah. I couldn't imagine losing Breonna so soon. We've only just begun."

"No need to be sorry. God has a plan, and it's being fulfilled. I'm just glad she's not suffering anymore. She's running around Heaven now, tumor-free. That's what I think about when I start to feel bad about it. I can't be selfish and wish her back."

"True. I'm just sad that Breonna might be going through this for my sake."

"I don't think she would be sad," Aaron suggested.

"Heh, she's not. I told her my feelings, and she said she was glad it happened to her if it drew me closer to God." Derrick pointed to Aaron. "Just as you said she would."

"Strong woman," Aaron said.

"Yes, sir," Derrick admitted, thinking of Breonna still laying in her hospital bed.

"I know the feeling," Aaron admitted with a smirk. Aaron lifted his cocoa mug. "To strong women!"

Derrick met his mug in the air and sipped the near-perfect chocolate drink. He stared at the cup savoring the flavor. "Another Deborah concoction?"

Aaron laughed after draining his mug. "Indeed it is. She is missed around here in more ways than one. I still haven't been able to nail that one all the time, either. She was the connoisseur's dream come true and their worst nightmare."

"How's that?"

"They love her cooking but can never exactly place what surprise ingredient she puts into it," Aaron shook his head. "And I'm one of them."

"I look forward to discovering those things about Breonna."

"You will, Derrick. Look and listen, and you will learn. Just don't take any moment for granted."

"I don't plan to." Derrick raised his mug, "Here's to the memory of love and the future of love."

Aaron lifted his empty mug and clapped it with Derrick's. Derrick set his mug down, picked up the key again, and wondered what secrets its destination held.

Chapter
Twenty-Eight

Derrick called the hospital to speak to Breonna, but he couldn't get through. They couldn't find her information. He didn't think she had her cell phone with her. He didn't even consider trying to call before leaving his house on Thanksgiving morning. He was due back at Davies Deli at 6 AM. By the time he arrived, Aaron and Pop were in full swing. Pop was shuffling around the kitchen, Aaron looked as if he hadn't left the night before, and a couple of students were arranging tables to fit larger groups. The smell of dressing grabbed him the moment he entered the building.

"Welcome back, Derrick," said the informed student with glasses. "I talked to my mom last night, and I described your key to her. She said that some boxes at her bank still use that type of key. She said for you to go in tomorrow morning, and she'd be happy to help you."

"Thank you for doing that. I appreciate it..." Derrick held out for a name.

"Ricky," he said. "My name is actually Richard, but my friends call me Ricky."

Derrick laughed. "There was a time when people used to call me Ricky. It's been a long time, though. Good to meet a fellow Ricky." Derrick reached out his hand, Ricky accepted it with a proud grin.

"Glad I could help," he said. "With your key being a mystery, I would sure like to know what you find. If you're able to say what's there, that is."

"I don't even know what to expect," Derrick said. "But you'll be one of the first I tell."

"Awesome, thanks," Ricky said and went back to rolling napkins around plasticware.

Aaron led him back into the kitchen where another group, this one much larger, were pulling trays out of the oven and placing them into tall warming cabinets.

"The cabinets are new. The company just dropped them off this morning, so keeping the backups warm will be much easier now than stacking them in the ovens. We have what's on the island and what we have in the warmers. The only things we need to make this morning are the vegetables and fresh rolls. The rolls don't take long, so we can make them as we go. Once we have a free oven, we'll get a couple of batches in."

"You really do have this organized," Derrick said.

"Heh, you should have seen us the first year. It was crazy. The second year we doubled in number. Crazy doesn't begin to explain. If it weren't for the donation of ovens, we couldn't have done it. This year, I just hope we've made enough."

"Sixteen hundred servings not enough?"

"I don't know what to expect. I let the Lord take care of that. I just serve up the meal, and whoever and however many show up is up to Him."

"Not to sound rude, but do we get to eat?" Derrick asked. He didn't want to chow down and then find out a needy person didn't get a meal.

"Oh yes, we'll get to eat. There's plenty for that. We each will take breaks throughout the day because it'll be a long one. We eat when we can."

Aaron led Derrick to where they had their butchering party. The area was clear of carcasses but now filled with warming cabinets and table steamers. The countertops were clean and ready for work.

"We thought about using Styrofoam containers, but to have a thousand of those? Pop didn't like the idea. We figured if we had a steady dishwasher, we could handle serving our meal on plates. It would also give those visiting another taste of home and not an impersonal container."

"Makes sense. It'll keep Peter busy, though," Derrick chuckled.

"Yeah, he'll have help. More of a runner to keep fresh plates with Pop. But we have plenty of plates so that it won't be too crazy for him."

"And the college students act as wait-staff as well?"

"We have four employees for that. You know Jasmine, but we'll have a couple more, yes. We need to keep the food running and be polite enough that when we see folks completing their meal, they understand there will be others waiting for a seat. That'll be one of the harder tasks because, for some, this is shelter."

Derrick thought back to the homeless crowd at the library. He wondered if he would see any of them here. He was taken back by how much thought Aaron and Pop had put into this place. It was right along where his heart was. Only the food he wanted to fill people with was education and the ability to get out of the situation that caused them to need this sort of facility. Still, he was happy to allow the less fortunate to experience a holiday meal and perhaps the love of family once again.

"Ever have any issues with anyone?"

"Not at all. Everyone is civil and behaves themselves. You get the occasional drunk who is a little loud or more reluctant to leave. We take that on a case-by-case basis."

"Ever evict someone?"

"No. Never. But there is always a first time. We just make sure we are aware of our surroundings and our company. Our arms are open for everyone, so we don't get any trouble."

Aaron finished his tour by showing him the front serving line where Jasmine set up the expeditors station. She had a couple of bins of Ricky-rolled plasticware.

"Just about set, boss," she said.

Derrick looked up at the illuminated clock with the Davies logo at its center. It was just before eight. Two hours to go before they opened the doors. He walked to the window, and Aaron pointed to an outside area that four students were roping off.

"That will be the walkway for people to enter—another oversight we made on the first meal. Now with a walkway cordoned off, the line will move more efficiently, and I won't get so much hate mail," he chuckled.

"Red carpet service," Derrick joked.

"Just efficient," Aaron sighed, "like Deborah would have had it. She was the queen of efficiency. Always making sure everything was in order."

"I didn't know her, but from what I've seen, I'm sure you would've made her proud."

"Thanks, Derrick," Aaron said, then breathed deeply. "Okay, let's show you where we will be." He crossed to the entrance. "With all the teens in the back with the food, I need someone out here with me to welcome people and usher them to tables. Jasmine will make sure the other servers help the bussers with clearing tables quickly, so we can bring in the next customers. We don't have to worry about a cashier because everyone eats free. There won't be a till in the register anyhow."

Aaron led him to a podium with a waist apron and a pad and pen. He handed them to Derrick. "You probably won't need to take any orders, but it's better to have it on you and not to need it than to need it and not have it."

Derrick took the apron and tied it around his waist. It barely fit. It was apparent they didn't have someone his size in mind when they made it. "So, how will the process go?"

"People walk in, you ask how many in their party, then you record it here," Aaron showed him a ledger that was on the podium. "We'll run it like a five-star restaurant. Take their name and number of people with them. If they don't want to give a name, find a characteristic that will distinguish them so we don't overlook anyone. Don't try to memorize anything. It's going to get hectic, and you'll get lost. Especially your first go around."

Derrick felt his nerves tense up. *What if I miss someone?* He thought. *Are there really going to be 2,000 people passing through the restaurant today?* He took a breath and released it. This was more intense than he'd anticipated.

"Don't worry,. You got this, Derrick. If you're going to be able to manage a bunch of rowdy teenagers, this should be a breeze."

An hour and a half later, Derrick looked out the same

window he had earlier, and this time the roped area had a decent line forming. It was an exciting sight. There people from were all walks of life standing patiently along the roped-off area. Derrick saw men and women like those laying around the library and those who worked in the city around them, talking and laughing like neighbors or even family. This was unlike the city where folks from these two walks of life would pretend the other didn't exist.

Derrick looked down at the empty ledger. There were enough slots to fill fifty names per page. This book would be ten to twenty pages deep by the end of the day. Filled with names that had faces behind them. It was the main thing they were driving home during his studies—that kids aren't conditions; they are people who need assistance. This was the whole reason he got into social work in the first place, for those with the faces like were outside. And he was reminded that adults also have needs and require the help of someone like him. When he looked back up the line had doubled in size; cars were pulling around the corner, trying to find a spot.

Aaron came from the kitchen, his hands jingling with a set of keys. He patted Derrick on the shoulder. "You ready for this?"

Derrick smiled with a newfound passion. "Let's do this."

Chapter
Twenty-Nine

It took a couple of pages before Derrick got comfortable with his customer logging system. He greeted them, took down their name and number in their party, and moved them to his left, where there was more room to wait. There were folding chairs and a waiting bench to sit on. Every chair remained full until one party's name was called, then the next batch would be seated. Derrick often glanced out the window, but the line never seemed to deminish. After two hours, he stopped looking.

With the limited seating, Aaron told him that booths would be for larger parties and the folding tables they had set up would be for singles, as it would be easier to share space if it were cafeteria-style seating rather than asking strangers to share a booth. The wait-staff would be responsible for telling Derrick what was available, and he would run down his list to see who would fit where.

Derrick checked over his shoulder at the crowd in the restaurant. It was loud with conversation and laughter; the same voices he heard through the window now blended together in one harmonious chorus. Social status, color, creed, or age didn't define anyone at the moment. All that mattered was that they were being fed. And if it came down to it, he wondered if food became the ancillary benefit to the family atmosphere that everyone was experiencing.

After another two hours and another three pages, the line started to thin. Derrick looked out the window into the glare of the day, and he could at last see the end of the line. He felt a mix of relief and pain. Glad that it was almost over, but wondering how many more were still out there needed food, but unable to come. *What about them?*

A hand on his shoulder pulled Derrick from his daze. "We can only help those we are able to help," Aaron said.

"How did you—" Derrick began

"It's a question I've asked since day one. But if we are too concerned about those not here, we'll lose sight of those who are. If we forget them, then what are we doing?"

Derrick nodded. "I get it."

"You need anything? Something to drink?"

"Yes, please," Derrick said as a family of four exited the building, the glow of joy shining from their faces. He called the next party of four, and they followed a college student to their table.

"Amazing, right?" Aaron said. Derrick could see him glowing.

"I would never think of this being so huge."

"None of us did," Aaron explained. "That's the beauty of it. Well, maybe Pop. But he's always been the dreamer."

"You're right. I'm sure Deborah would be proud of what this has become."

Aaron brought his tea, and he sipped the dryness away. The tea was made just the way he liked it. He immediately thought of Jasmine. *This place knows its stuff,* he said to himself, then called the next batch of hungry customers.

Around 5:00, the line became shorter. Derrick could barely see any people in line. The outdoor roped area was clear. It would be getting dark soon, and he felt those who were coming had already been through. He would love to do the math and see a final number, but to count to 2,000 was not something he was interested in doing. If anything, it had felt like 10,000 had passed by him. He suddenly felt exhausted. He was amazed he hung on so long. Usually, he couldn't stand around too long with his size, but here he was, seven hours later and going strong.

Another six left the deli, and another six replaced them. Jasmine took the family to their table. Derrick checked his list and marked the family off, and without looking up said, "May I have your name and how many in your group, please?"

"Greene, party of four."

Derrick looked up and saw that familiar voice was attached to an even more familiar smile.

"Breonna?" Derrick asked, almost speechless. "What are you doing here?"

Breonna smirked. "I heard this was a good place to eat."

"But you—" Derrick began but couldn't finish. Thinking of what she must've gone through to make the trip.

"I'm fine. And it's good to see you too," she said in her snarky tone.

Derrick shook the cobwebs from his head. "I'm sorry, yes, it's great to see you. All of you," Derrick said, taking in the whole family. "Let me write you down, and we'll call your name as soon as a table is ready."

"Thanks," Breonna said. Her parents snickered at their interaction.

Derrick took the next couple of names and, like all the others, let them know they would be seated as soon as there was room. Once complete, he stepped around the podium and went to the family.

"So, they just let you go?"

"It took some bribery and a firm discussion from my dad here," Breonna said, thumbing over to him.

"They said you were okay to leave," Mr. Greene said. "We weren't going to miss Thanksgiving with the family because of overprotective doctors."

"I'm glad you could make it. It's nice to be with family," Derrick returned the stare.

Derrick felt the brush of another family leaving the deli. He turned and thanked them for coming and added that he hoped he'd see them again soon. He turned back to the Greenes, "One of the waitresses will be over here soon to take you back to your table," Derrick said. "I gotta get back to work. I'm happy you're here, Breonna. It's good to see you up and around."

One of the teens took the Greenes back to their table. Derrick crossed their name off and wrote down the next couple of families.

A few minutes later, Derrick felt a familiar tap on his shoulder, "Derrick. Is that Breonna and her family? She's here?"

"Yes. She was released from the hospital early and came to eat."

Aaron laughed. "You still don't get it."

"Get what?"

"They're here for you, not the meal."

"Even if they are, we still have a line to get through."

"Nuh-huh. I can take over from here. You've done exceptional. Now you need to spend with your family." Aaron pointed toward where they were sitting.

"Are you sure?" Derrick asked, not wanting to sound too eager.

"If you don't go, then you're fired," Aaron said, holding out his hand. "Your apron and pen, please, sir." Aaron grinned and raised his eyebrows.

Derrick looked toward the line. The thinned crowd was now only within the outer lobby, but one person stood out. It was Clarence, the Davies Deli veteran. He had a smile from ear to ear. "You better listen to him, kiddo. She ain't gonna wait forever."

Derrick didn't need any other invitations. He handed Aaron his apron and grinned. "Sorry it couldn't work out, sir."

Derrick waded around a waitress with a drink order, another with hot turkey and dressing plates, and one emptying a booth. He could see the family in the back and made his way to them. Breonna had her back to him, but Mr. and Mrs. Greene had a full view of his approach. Both had smiles on their faces.

As he was within earshot, he heard her question her parent's expressions. "What?" she said.

Derrick placed his hand on her shoulder, "I hear this place has a pretty good Spaghetti Sub. You should try it."

Breonna took the back of his hand and held it to her cheek. "I'm glad you could make it. I was praying you'd come." She kissed his hand and released it.

"I'm here. This is where I should be," Derrick said.

Jasmine came up to them with a chair, "Here ya go. Sure beats standing."

Derrick thanked her and sat at the head of the booth.

"And the sub?" Breonna smiled. "Not on your life."

The family laughed at his expense, which felt good. He was grateful for their acceptance and for them being comfortable enough to let loose around him.

Jasmine returned and took everyone's drink order and choice of vegetable. After another ten minutes, they were eating Thanksgiving dinner as a family. Something that Derrick knew would be an experience he would carry for the rest of his life—or if things progressed as everyone around them was inferring, an experience he would remember for the rest of their life together.

After the meal, Derrick walked the family out to their car. Breonna had a pronounced limp but seemed okay otherwise. She was her usual talkative self throughout dinner. If her facial bruising and cast weren't so prominent, it would be hard to tell she had been in a major accident just days before. He again thanked God for His protection and for Breonna so strong through it all.

Mr. Greene came around the vehicle and stuck out his hand. "Tell your friend he is doing something amazing here. It was a blessing to be part of it. And thank you for being there for Breonna. It means a lot to her, and it meant a lot to us."

Derrick accepted the handshake and compliment. "You're welcome, sir. And thank you, I'll pass your message on to Aaron and Mr. Davies."

Derrick watched as the Greenes pulled away. He looked at the deli and thought back to his first drive up to the place. It seemed much bigger now than it did then. It made him think about how perceptions often spoil what we find on the inside. It wasn't only the building that seemed bigger. It was the heart of those inside it that made the difference.

Chapter
Thirty

Derrick walked back into the diner with a pep in his step. Not only from their meal but what he had learned during it. During dinner Derrick had explained to the Greenes what he discovered about the key and how Ricky learned it was to a safety deposit box. Derrick told them of his plans to visit the bank the following day to speak with a banker about accessing the box. He asked for prayer because of his previous issues with the bank account and the possibility that his name may not be on the safety deposit box because it hadn't been on any of the other accounts his mom had.

Breonna asked to go, but from the disapproving glances from her parents, he could tell they felt it was too soon for her to be out and about. He told her he would love for her to go but that she needed her rest and that he would be heading straight to the bank after work and cutting it close to closing time. She relented but asked for a play-by-play report. He had agreed.

Derrick reentered the restaurant, still overwhelmed with how busy it had been. Now, just a couple of families, several singles, and the Davies Deli staple, Clarence, were left in the deli. Derrick walked to his booth and introduced himself. "Hello, sir. My name is Derrick. I just wanted to tell you, Happy Thanksgiving."

"I know who you are, young man. Gary speaks of you all the time."

Taken back, Derrick sat across from Clarence. "How do you know Gary?"

"We served together," he said and went back to his coffee.

"Wow. Small world. We only officially met about a week ago, and he told me about his experiences overseas."

"Is that right?" Clarence took another long drink of his coffee. He didn't have the reflective expression that Gary did.

Derrick quickly realized what Gary meant when he mentioned that some guys came back different and that their experiences usually weren't good ones. Gary said he was one of the lucky ones. From the look on Clarence's face, his memories of the war weren't pleasant. He didn't know how to proceed. But if he did learn anything the past couple of weeks, it was that adults were no different from the teens he was studying to help.

"I can see that you and he may have different perspectives on what happened over there," Derrick said.

Clarence emptied his cup and with glassy eyes, nodded. "You could say that."

"Have you ever spoken about your experiences? Good or bad?"

"No need to. They happened. Nothing can change that."

"True, but whatever you're carrying, sometimes it's good to talk about it. May give you some peace about what you went through," Derrick said.

Jasmine came and refilled Clarence's cup and set down a tea for Derrick. She smiled and winked as she walked away.

Clarence didn't bother to sugar or cream his coffee, just sipped it as it was. "As you can figure, Gary isn't the only one to see action. He was one of the lucky ones. To walk away from a roadside bomb, that's a miracle. The others who were in that Humvee with him were not so lucky. There are way too many folded flags sitting on bookshelves and mantles today."

Derrick understood there were two sides to war. The experiences of the good you did, as Gary had. But then there were the negative experiences. The ones who bore the scars of what happened; the ones who had nightmares about the men and women who were lost. He had learned Gary's story. Now with Clarence, he was hearing the darker side. The man who was wounded by his memories of war.

"Were you injured over there?"

Clarence looked down at his cup and rotated it with his hands. "Physically? Nope."

"Well, that's something to be thankful for. God had his hand on you," Derrick tried to give the man in front of him some hope. But it had little effect. He just stared at his coffee.

"I don't know what to think. I was in charge over many of them. I was in the Humvee two vehicles back from the IUD that killed most of our team." Clarence looked down and shook his head, "Something didn't feel right that morning. I should've paid more attention to my gut than to orders printed on paper from someone miles away from the threat."

"And Gary was on your team?"

Clarence nodded. "He was in the vehicle in front of me. It didn't get hit by the blast but by shrapnel. That's what injured Gary, but I'm sure he has told you that much."

"Yes, sir. He has. You must be Sarge. He told me a guy he called Sarge saved his life. He speaks highly of you. That should count for something. You were able to save his life, and he was able to come home because of you."

Clarence again nodded, this time with tears. He continued to sip his coffee in silence. Only a few stragglers remained in the diner as Clarence emptied his cup.

"Well, Derrick. I must be going. I'm meeting Gary. We're going to watch the game."

Derrick stood with him and reached out his hand. Clarence took it. "It was a pleasure meeting you. I'll be praying for you," Derrick said. He hoped he would remember his promise.

Clarence left a tip on the table and headed toward the door where Jasmine met him, locking the door behind him.

"I see you met Clarence," Aaron said, coming up to him from the kitchen.

"Yeah. You said he was a regular here. The girls said he never has visitors or speaks much."

"Not really, but he's a nice guy. You sure got him to open up."

"We have a common friend, it seems. That was the door to get him to talk," Derrick explained, but he wouldn't go into details

"No. I think it's more you have a way with people. It's why you're going to make an excellent social worker. You see people and want to help them. They're not just a number or statistic with you."

Derrick nodded. It was the way he had always been. He couldn't understand how people could interact without going deeper, especially when that was the purpose of the con-nection. The kids he would see would be more than names and numbers. Seeing people now and the adults he had encountered helped him realize that his interaction with younger adults would impact who they became as adults. He suddenly felt the weight of the world.

By the time Derrick pushed through the swinging door, the college helpers had most of the kitchen clean. Peter was standing in a cloud of spray and steam, finishing the final stacks of dishes in front of him. He realized his job was probably the most difficult of them all. Another reminder of the youth he was preparing to help. They could be the unsung heroes; they needed to be happy with who they were, not who they aspired to be. A dishwasher could be just as inspiring as a waiter or a cook.

Derrick looked around the kitchen. The bins that had lined the kitchen were now reduced to a pan and a half of turkey and a pan of dressing. Each vegetable pan was only about half-full.

Aaron came up beside him. He nodded to the one table with the few pans on it. "We barely had enough. That's all that's left."

"I don't know what to say." Derrick stood amazed. Amazed at what he had been through, amazed at how everyone worked together, amazed at how God orchestrated it all.

"Amazing, right?"

Derrick had to laugh, "Yes, that it was. I've never experienced anything like that before."

"Well, now that you have, will you be coming back next year?" Aaron patted Derrick on the shoulder and laughed.

Derrick nodded, joining him in the amusement. "Most definitely."

"Let's get this place cleaned up and get out of here."

Derrick pitched in with the crew that was wiping down

tables, vacuuming, and returning the place back to sitting order. After another hour, the students headed back home, to apartments, or their dorm. Jasmine was rinsing the coffee pot and wiping down the final counter of the evening. It was quiet in the kitchen, which meant even Peter was done with the dishes. Derrick could only imagine how tired he must be.

They were the last four in the diner. Pop had left shortly after the doors closed. There were few leftovers. All the team had taken a to-go box with them, leaving only half a bin of turkey. Aaron said that Mom used to make pot pies with the remaining turkey. He would look into that in the morning.

Aaron locked the doors behind them with their boxes in hand and sighed. Exhausted? Maybe. But from the look on his face, it was more than that. He missed Deborah. Derrick thought of Breonna, grateful he hadn't lost her.

As if she had heard his thoughts, Derrick's phone rang. He looked at the display and smiled. It was her.

Aaron grinned at his sudden change in demeanor. "Breonna?"

"Yeah," Derrick said.

Aaron waved goodbye and headed to his Jeep. Derrick slow-paced to his car, talking to the one everyone was sure was for him. His guard still gave him warning but was finally breaking down. He loved her, but he wanted to make sure it wasn't a heat of the moment reaction or the pressure of those around them. If he were to take any steps closer to Breonna, he had to know for sure it was the right thing to do.

Derrick fell asleep wondering about Clarence and woke on Friday morning with Gary on his mind. After a quick shower and trim, he headed to the restaurant. He looked around upon entering the place, expecting to see the familiar service cap and a mound of sugar wrappers next to a creamer bin. Instead, a young couple sat in Gary's usual spot enjoying their breakfast.

Derrick double-checked his phone to see if he had the right time. It was still well before nine. Gary should still be in his seat sipping coffee and spouting off about how poorly the Rockets had played the night before. But he wasn't there. Derrick scanned the restaurant to see if he had sat elsewhere, but there was no sign of a military cap.

Not knowing what else to do, he approached the counter. "I'll take two bacon, egg, and cheese tacos and a tea." The cashier wrote his ticket and put it in the window. "You know what, make it a coffee instead." For some reason, he just craved the drink this morning.

Once he was handed his cup, he creamed and sugared it, and returned the lid. A couple of sips later, he felt energized and wondered why he hadn't picked up the beverage sooner. A couple of minutes later, the cashier handed him his tacos, but curiosity got the better of him.

"Say, the gentleman who usually sits over there," he head nodded to the couple, "Gary. Has he been in today? Did I miss him?"

The waitress' gaze fell to the ground. "Oh yes, Mr. Fletcher. So sad."

"Sad? What happened?"

"Mr. Fletcher passed away." She turned to another server. "When did Mr. Fletcher pass away?"

"Last night," the other said.

"Yes. Apparently, he had a heart attack at his home, and by the time they reached him, it was too late."

"Are you serious?"

"I wish I were joking. But he's gone," the waitress said. "You're Derrick, aren't you?"

Almost nervous to answer because of their conversation, "Yeah. I'm Derrick."

"There was a man named Clarence in here this morning, looking for you. He's the one who told us. He said he and Mr. Fletcher were friends."

"Yeah, they were," Derrick said, not sure what else to say.

"He talked about you," the waitress beamed.

"I'm sorry?"

"Mr. Fletcher. Especially after you had breakfast with him last week." The waitress looked at him as if he were a celebrity. "He has never talked to us that much. He's been in here almost every morning for the last year, and the first thing he asks is, *Has Derrick been in yet?* Some days you two would talk, others it was a quick, *Hello.* He would soon leave after you passed through. It was good to see you two finally get the time to sit down together. How long have you known him?"

Derrick didn't know how to respond. Gary had been looking for human contact, and the one person he was hoping to get it from kept passing him by every morning. He wondered how the connection between them cemented in his mind. Was it the simple sports talk on how bad or good the Rockets were doing? It couldn't be that simple, could it? Every day he studied the strength of human contact and how the teens he soon would be helping were starving for it. But was Gary just as hungry? Was Clarence?

"He was a friend. I only wish I had known him better," Derrick said, then raised his taco bag. "Thank you, Theresa. You have a good day."

Chapter
Thirty-One

The bank was busy with customers when Derrick arrived after the end of his shift. The teller line nearly reached the door. It made him glad his destination was a banker and not a teller. He went to the podium to sign in and saw he was fifth in line. Every one of the four offices was occupied. Derrick figured it wouldn't take too long to be seen. He wrote down his name, almost writing a '1' next to his name out of habit. The thought made him laugh.

Derrick watched the teller line thin and swell. Bankers steadily checked off names ahead of his, and the manager danced between the two. A signature here, and a key turn there, kept her heels *click-clacking* on the tile floor. He wondered which had it better, the manager dividing her time or the tellers who had to stand and deal with less than happy customers at the length of the line.

The teller line had been through two cycles of him marking the last person in line and reaching a teller. His line had shrunk down to him and the name above his. Every time he saw a banker leave their office, he perked up, but half the time they were heading back to the manager's office or to the teller line to conduct a customer's transaction.

Breonna messaged him twice. Once to say good morning, the other to see if they could get together after he got finished at the bank. He had to admit his stomach tumbled when his phone buzzed with each notification. He was rereading her recent text, imagining the smile behind it when his name was called. He almost missed it.

"Mr. Anders?" the banker called a second time.

Derrick shot up. "Right here, sorry."

"My name is Emily. I will be your banker this afternoon. Follow me, please." She extended her hand toward her office door.

"Good afternoon, Emily," Derrick said, following her to an office that had plenty of children's pictures—mostly baby. *She must be a new mother*, Derrick thought.

"Cute kid," Derrick said, thumbing toward the collage she had on a shelf.

Emily beamed, "Thank you, Mr. Anders. I appreciate it. She's our first. Guess I can't get enough photos."

"Please, call me Derrick. It must be difficult to be away."

"Yes, but we all have to work. So, Derrick, how can I help you today?"

Derrick fished the key out of his pocket and set it on Emily's desk. "I need to access my mother's safety deposit box. I'm hoping it's here, because this is where she did her banking."

Emily picked up the key. "Well, this is an older key. We changed our boxes a little over a year ago. As each customer came in, we switched over to the new ones." Emily reached into her desk. "Do you have a key that looks like this?" she held out a flat key with a couple of teeth on the end. There aren't too many that still have this older key."

"No, I don't. My mother passed away a few years ago. She's banked here for years, and I do my banking here. But I've been unable to access her accounts because I'm not listed on them."

"Unfortunately, with the key, the same situation would apply," Emily began, a true empathetic tone in her voice, not coarse as the others had gotten before. "I can look up the box for you, but if the key is tied to any of her accounts, or doesn't have you listed on them, then there will be nothing I can do for you."

Derrick sighed. "Please. I need to see what's in that box. It could be the information you are looking for. My mom died suddenly and was never able to pass on any information about the home we live in, our mortgage, let alone this key that I didn't know existed until the day before yesterday."

"I'm sorry, Derrick. The most I can do for you is look up your mom's name to see if you're on the account. If you aren't, we cannot give you access. Just understand it's not that we don't want to help, it's that we—"

"Cannot help. Yeah, I've heard the song and dance," Derrick took a breath. "Sorry. I don't mean any offense. I've just heard it all the last three years. I know the law bind you."

"Let's just see what this key holds?" Emily began to research information on his mother's account again. She shook her head several times. She looked up at Derrick to see his confusion.

"Sorry, I do that. It means nothing. I'm just reviewing what we already know and trying to find if we missed anything. So far, it's all the same. But I'm not giving up."

"What about the key?"

"I don't seem to see it in her file here. I can tell you that much. Her account with us does not include a safety deposit box."

"But this is your bank's key, right?"

Emily picked up the key and examined it. "I believe so. I've only been here two years, these keys were from before my time, but they do look familiar." Emily stood. "I'm going to go check with another banker who has been here almost ten years. If anyone will know, it's her."

Derrick sat back in the quiet office. Emily's baby stared at him from the photos on her bookshelf. One was of her husband and their baby. It reminded him of the picture of him and his father in his wallet. It took him back to when all of this started. A simple book that his mom would read to him. Maybe that's why the photo was there. A little reminder to her that she once loved two men. The man who gave her the son he held, and the man who loved to read. Did she know that he was an angel? Or is that why he left, because he could never really be with her?

"I have an answer for you, Derrick," Emily said, startling Derrick out of his reverie. She had a huge smile on her face. Good news? "It turns out this *is* one of our keys." Emily turned on a desk lamp and turned it toward Derrick, handing him the key. "If you look here, you can faintly see a serial number."

Sure enough, it was faint, but the purple etching could be made out under the lamp's bright light. "And you found out something?"

"The key is in your name, Mr. Anders," Emily said.

"I'm sorry? Did you say it's in my name?"

"Yes, sir. The box was purchased four years ago. Since the

keys are only switched out as the customer comes in for switching, this one was never converted."

"I don't understand. How can the box be in my name?"

"That's how your mother set it up. She is the primary, but you're the secondary. With her passing, the box automatically becomes yours. You have free access to it. All I need is to see your ID, and I can take you back to the box."

Derrick couldn't believe it. His mom had arranged for a safety deposit box for him before she died. Or maybe she intended to before she passed, but the accident cut things short. He wondered why she never told him. Well, there were many things she never told him.

"Can I take you to your box, Derrick?"

"Yes, most certainly. Do I need to sign anything?"

"Just that you're accessing your box. For your records and for ours." She made a couple of clicks on her keyboard and turned a signature pad toward him. "Sign in the window there, and we can take you back. All this is is confirmation that you are accessing your safety deposit box today."

Derrick's hand was shaking as he signed his name. He was finally about to get at least some answers about his mom.

"Okay. Follow me." Emily stood and led him past the gate and into the vault. She directed him to the area where boxes lined the wall. There were different sizes and shapes. "Yours is SJ279. It's the third row all the way down."

Derrick walked to the box and looked at the numbers, then the key, then back to Emily.

Emily inserted her key, then turned to Derrick. "Just insert your key and turn it."

Derrick turned his key, and Emily turned hers. The door swung open, and Emily pulled out the box and shut the door, removing her key; Derrick did the same. Emily took the box to a table in the center of the vault and set it down.

"Okay. I will leave the two of you alone," she said with a smile. "I'll come back and check on you in about ten minutes."

Emily left, and Derrick could only stare at the box. His past and future were inside. He was almost too nervous to open it, but he needed to. The latch released easily, and Derrick opened the lid. Inside were several envelopes, each one had a label written in his mother's handwriting. The thick one read *Family Photos*. The title itself frightened him. Since he could remember, there had never been a family—just him and his mom. He unfolded the tabs and opened the envelope.

Inside were photos of him and his mom. He found Kinder photos, grade school, and some high school photographs. Most were of him, but many were of him and his mom. A second envelope fell out of the larger one. This one was labeled, *Derrick, Sr.* Derrick almost choked. *I'm a junior?* That was one thing that his mom never mentioned—his father's name. It was always *your dad* this or *your father* that. He never had a name, now he did, and it was his own. He now understood why she would call him Ricky. It could have done with the pain of losing her first Derrick. The thick envelope contained dozens of photos of him and his dad, including a larger version of the one he found in the book. Photos of his dad feeding him, photos of him being changed, even photos of the three of them together. His family suddenly became real.

Derrick set down the photos and picked up the second envelope labeled *House Documents*.

Could this be? Derrick thought.

He unfolded the pins and pulled out the mortgage

paperwork for the house. It had his mom's name on it, but not his, as the bankers and tellers would always tell him. Inside was also the payment schedule for the mortgage, those drafts that always occurred on the 12th of the month. Each one was spelled out. But what he found odd was that the payment schedule ended almost a year ago.

Was the house paid off?

The third was an envelope labeled *Morrison, Mueller, and Associates.* It was his mom's will. It was dated shortly before that night with her and Carter. Was this one of the things they argued about? Could this box be part of it? It suddenly occurred to him that Carter had made sure Breonna got that purse.

If he is who Aaron says he is, he knew the key was there all along.

He thumbed through the will. He was no attorney, but it looked like his mom left him the house, a bank account, and other personal items. But the house was the biggest. He could get what he needed to access the bank account that paid the mortgage with this document.

The final envelope was standard letter-sized. It didn't have a label. But he knew what it was before opening it. It was the letter that explained everything. It would tell him what he had been desperately seeking for three years. But most of all, it would be the final words he would hear from his mom.

Chapter
Thirty-Two

My dearest Derrick.

I cannot begin to express how much I love you. You mean the world to me, and I'm blessed to be your mother. If you are reading this, I've passed on. With a little bit of luck, I am walking through a heavenly garden with your father. By now, you should know you bear his name. I ask for your forgiveness for shutting him out of your life for so long. I never talked about him because of the pain it caused me. Then it just became second nature to talk about him in passing. I never brought him up because I believed you were uncomfortable talking about him. I was wrong. It was me who was uncomfortable. I did you a disservice by not letting you get to know the man I loved and married.

I don't want you to start thinking that your father ran off and left us alone to fend for ourselves. I know that's the impression you got from me with my silence. But your father was an honorable man. And he loved me, and he loved you. You can tell by the grin on his face each time he held you. That's why it was so painful when God took him from us. That's why I've been so bitter about anything spiritual. Your father loved God with all he was. And I was angry for a long time because why would God take someone away from a new family who loved Him so much?

Today, as I write this to you, I understand things better. Last week I met a man who has changed my life. His name is Carter. While I never introduced him to you, please understand that he was a big part of my life. He was the one who was important to me coming back to God. But everything changed. I went to the doctors for headaches, and they went ahead and showed me a cancer diagnosis. I am dying, sweetie. I don't know how much I have left. But if you're reading this, it's because I'm gone, or I'm too far gone to make decisions for myself. Either way, you need to be the man of the house now, not that you never weren't. I guess you've filled those shoes for years.

All the documents you need to take over the house and finances are here, and I've included some memories of your father. I can only ask your forgiveness they weren't given to you sooner. In protecting my pain, I caused you so much.

I don't know what circumstances you will be under when you receive this letter—grieving most likely. But remember that I love you and always will.

Mom

P.S. If you ever come across a striking gentleman in a tweed coat and hat, that's Carter. Treat him well because he saved me, in more ways than one. And I can honestly say that he could've been the only man I've ever loved besides your father.

Derrick took a deep breath and wiped the tears from his eyes. Emily had not returned. He allowed himself to let go. It was the first time he cried over his mom's death. Her letter indicated she no clue of what was about to happen to her. She was more concerned about his comfort and him understanding about her life, their life. Derrick closed his eyes and prayed. First, asking for forgiveness for judging anyone, his mom or Carter. He prayed, thanking God for his provision throughout his life. He never wanted, and God must have had something to do with that. Finally, he prayed for strength to continue. His life had been so complicated, and now that he was at a junction point, he wanted to be on God's side instead of his own.

As Derrick was thanking God, a small tap echoed in the room. "Mr. Anders. Are you okay? May I come in?"

Derrick took a deep breath and exhaled. "Certainly, Emily. I have what I came for. I can take everything, correct?"

"Yes, sir, the box belongs to you."

"Thank you." Derrick took the mortgage, the will, and the banking files and closed the box.

Emily led Derrick to place the box back into the slot. They both turned their keys. "I can have the locksmith come out next week and change out the keys if you'd like."

Derrick held the key. It felt part of him now, "I'd like to hold onto it for a bit if you don't mind."

Emily smiled. "Certainly, sir. Is there anything else I can help you with?"

"Yes. I need to set an appointment with a banker. I have an account I'd like to access," Derrick smiled, waving the envelopes in his hand.

Epilogue

Four weeks later

"**B**reonna, are you almost ready?" Derrick called from the living room.

"You try and brush our hair with one hand and see how long it takes you, mister," Breonna teased. She entered looking stunning, taking Derrick's breath away, as usual.

"Do we really need to go to this?" she pouted.

"Come on. It'll be fun. I know you're still a bit shy about singing in front of me, but this is just Christmas caroling. No one expects you to sing well."

Breonna punched him with her good fist. "Just wait until I get out of this cast, buster. You'll think twice about your wisecracks."

Derrick leaned over and kissed her, this time on the lips. Both had returned to their original caramel color, and she was no longer limping. Her only complaint was the cast that the doctors said would be on into the new year.

Breonna had attended his church the week after

Thanksgiving. To Derrick's surprise, she fell in love with the church, and the church fell in love with her.

Breonna said she had always wanted to find a small church, that she felt lost within her family's big church. The lack of TV screens and speakers only enamored her more to the idea. They had been regular attenders ever since—best of all, with her parent's blessing.

The Carols and Candles service was Calhaven Baptist's tour of local facilities to sing Christmas carols for shut-ins and nursing home residents, and they made a stop in a couple of shopping malls to bring cheer to their community.

Derrick had a meeting on Monday with the bank to finalize the paperwork on the house. It turned out that the paperwork was correct. He had paid off the house a year before, but for some inexplicable reason, the bank had kept making payments. They credited his account for the entire year of house payments plus interest, with the sincerest of apologies. The funds were deposited back into the previously locked account that he now had full access to due to his mom's recently discovered will. He learned that his mother had been an excellent steward of their finances. Even without to windfall from the excess mortgage payments, Derrick would be more than financially stable.

It had been a long month for both of them. Between schooling and working their shifts at the bookstore, they had little time to spend together. This caroling was more of a date than an opportunity to sing with the choir.

But cookies and cocoa, Derrick thought. *Who could pass that up?*

"You tricked me, Gabriel," the tweed-capped angel said to the ball-capped angel sitting in the park.

"Who me? Whenever have I done such a thing?"

"Nearly every time I have a case, there is always something to it that you leave out," Carter said, scooping a bite out of the cup he held.

"What's that you have there?"

"It's called *Gelato*. It's fabulous. You want a bite?" Carter held out a spoonful to Gabriel, who turned his head away.

"I'll stick to Jell-O, thank you."

"Why weren't you upfront about this case from the get-go. Things would've gone much smoother than they did."

"Would you have taken the case if I *had* told you?"

Carter sat silent and took another scoop of his snack. "Probably not. But still, that doesn't mean it's okay to throw me into the deep end."

"But it worked, and Derrick has now made reconciliation. About his mom, his father, and you for that matter," Gabriel said, pointing to him.

"All's well that ends well," Carter tipped his cap. "We make a good team, you and I, Gabe."

"I wouldn't have to look like this," Gabriel pointed to his disguise of ball cap and Dallas Cowboy's windbreaker.

"You know you look silly in that," Carter said, nodding to Gabriel's cap. "Seriously, you don't want be seen with that Cowboy's get-up in this part of the state."

"Civilian clothes work for you."

"Ah, that is because I am me. The vagabond look is distinguishing on me," Carter adjusted the lapels of his coat, pulling on them like suspenders.

Gabriel looked Carter up and down.

"It *does* work for you. I'll give you that."

"Thank you." Carter sighed. "I mean it. Thank you. If it weren't for you, I would've never completed this assignment."

Gabriel nodded. "You're welcome. Just don't let it happen again."

Carter looked up from his empty gelato cup. "You mean all is forgiven? He won't hold this against me?"

"That's what He does, Carter. Forgiveness is who God is. No matter how bad you may mess things up," Gabriel poked him in the shoulder.

"Well, that I do appreciate. It won't happen again," Carter said.

"I'm sure it won't," Gabriel said, eyeing his companion.

They watched a child chase after a butterfly around their family's picnic blanket.

"So, where do we go from here?" Carter asked.

"That's up to you. Are you ready for another assignment so soon?"

"I need to keep busy. One can only read for so long."

"Carter Jennings, are you saying you're getting tired of books?"

"Not at all. I'm just saying I'd rather live them."

"How is this for living?" Gabriel produced another shoebox, just the kind Carter liked to use, and handed it to him. "Have you ever read Charles Dickens?"

"You mean?" Carter said, taking a peek inside the shoebox and quickly shutting it. "Are you serious?"

"I am an angel of the Lord. I'm always serious." Gabriel stood and removed his cap and jacket. A flash of light surrounded him as his angelic appearance was restored. He gazed at Carter through crystal blue eyes.

"One day, you're going to have to teach me how you do that," Carter said.

Gabriel laughed. Even his laughter sounded heavenly. "What do you say, Carter. You up for *this* adventure?"

Carter looked again into the shoebox and grinned "I wouldn't miss it for the world."

About the Author

Jeff S. Bray lives in a small town in South Central Texas with his wife Carolyn and two of their five children. They are members of the local First Baptist Church, serving in several capacities, including teaching Sunday School, working with Men's Ministry, and managing the church's online presence.

Jeff's passion for writing began in elementary school with a short story about a lost kitten. His circuitous literary career started with his personal blog, *Moments for the Heart*, which led to small paid assignments before expanding into magazine articles in national publications.

Little Reminders of Who I Was, is the sequel to the supernatural romance, *Little Reminders of Who I Am*. Jeff is also the author of the contemporary thrillers *The Transference* and *The Five Barred Gate*, and the whimsical children's picture book series, *Elissa the Curious Snail*, which helps parents introduce basic faith concepts like prayer, even in the face of adversity, into their teachings in a fun and entertaining way.

Connect with Jeff online at:

jeffsbrayauthor.com

Also Available From
WordCrafts Press

The Carpenter and His Bride
by Paula K. Parker

Oh, to Grace!
by Abby Rosser

Paint Me Fearless
by Hallie Lee

In Search of the Beloved
by Marian Rizzo

www.WordCrafts.net

www.ingramcontent.com/pod-product-compliance
Lightning Source LLC
Chambersburg PA
CBHW050837190726
48286CB00007B/2120